Boyds will Be Boyds™

Get Well Soon or Else!

MVFOL

D0181242

Cover illustration by Serge Bloch

ISBN 0-439-57470-6

12 11 10 9 8 7 6 5 4 3 2 1   5 6 7 8 9/0

Printed in the U.S.A.   40
First printing, March 2004

Boyds will Be Boyds™

GET WELL SOON OR ELSE!

by sarah weeks

AN
APPLE
PAPERBACK

SCHOLASTIC INC.
New York Toronto London Auckland Sydney
Mexico City New Delhi Hong Kong Buenos Aires

For Lannie Rosenfield

— S.W.

CHAPTER ONE

"Do you think we're going to have to see Mrs. West in her nightgown?" asked Fink as we walked to school together one morning.

"I sure hope not," I said.

Mrs. West is our fifth-grade teacher. She's okay as a teacher, but that doesn't mean I want to see what she sleeps in at night.

"She's not going to be staying in our cabin with us, is she?" he asked.

"Of course not. She'll sleep with the girls," I said.

"So is Mr. Galluzzi sleeping in our cabin?" Fink said. "'Cause I definitely don't want to see *him* in a nightgown!"

I laughed. Mr. Galluzzi is our gym teacher. He's kind of big around the middle and except for the fact that he's totally bald, he's by far the hairiest person I've ever seen. He's even got hair growing out of his ears. The thought of him in a nightgown, especially a frilly one with flowers all over it like the kind my mom wears, was too much.

"I hope there won't be a lot of sports at nature camp," Fink said. "That summer my parents sent me to sleepaway camp, all we did all day long was play sports."

"Oh, yeah, I remember. You weren't allowed to play because your mom wrote one of her notes, right?" I asked.

My mom says that Fink's parents are "a tad overprotective." Actually, they're nuts. Especially about sports. They're afraid Fink's going to get hurt and I don't really get it, because Fink isn't a klutz or anything. But his mother is always writing these notes saying that he's not allowed to participate in anything "sports-related."

"That summer, her note was totally over the top,"

Fink told me. "It said I wasn't allowed to play anything that involved a ball, a bat, a stick, a racket, a puck, or a paddle. That pretty much covered it. So I spent the whole two months in the arts and crafts cabin making key chains. Hundreds of them. I've got a lifetime supply if you ever need one."

Fink and I get along great. We've been best friends since kindergarten. We spend as much time together as possible, which is pretty easy for us because we only live a few houses apart on the same street. We have tons of sleepovers, and we walk to and from school together every day. But on weekends I play soccer in the fall, basketball in the winter, and baseball in the spring, and all Fink is allowed to play is the clarinet. Don't tell him I said this, but when he plays, it sounds pretty bad.

"I wouldn't worry too much about the sports thing, Fink," I told him. "I think it's probably called *nature* camp for a reason. We'll be doing nature stuff."

Nature camp is a fifth-grade tradition at our school. Every year the fifth grade gets to miss a whole week of school and go to camp together for five days.

Our teachers are the counselors, and there are no parents on the trip. Fink and I had been looking forward to this since the minute we found out about it.

"What kind of nature stuff do you think we'll be doing?" asked Fink.

"I don't know, probably taking hikes, and looking at leaves and birds and stuff like that," I said.

"That sounds okay," he said, "unless there are mosquitoes. I don't know why, but for some reason those little buzzards just can't get enough of me. I must taste sweet or something."

"Yeah, or something," I said. "Just make sure to pack some bug spray, and you'll be fine."

"That stuff doesn't work on me. No matter how much of it I put on, they can still smell me right through it," he said. "Sort of like you and your Manly Mint."

Fink was talking about my deodorant. It's called Manly Mint and it's supposed to keep you from having B.O., but not long ago I discovered (the hard way) that it doesn't always work.

"If your bug spray doesn't work, don't worry. I can

always take care of those pesky mosquitoes by slapping them for you, like this —" I said, whacking Fink playfully a few times on the top of the head.

"Gee, thanks," he said, pushing me away. "That's very thoughtful of you, Nat-Man."

We got to the schoolyard with plenty of time to spare before the first bell.

"Ugh. Check out the Red Devils," Fink said, jabbing me in the ribs with his elbow and pointing toward the front door.

The Red Devils is our nickname for Marla Dundee and her evil twin, Jessie Kornblume, also known as Corn Bloomers. Even though Jessie and Marla are both short and have red hair, freckles, and beady little eyes, they're not really twins. They're just so much alike it seems as though they are. Fink and I can't stand them, and they feel exactly the same way about us, but we're all in the same class so we have to see each other every single day whether we like it or not.

"I'm so glad I'm not a girl," Fink said.

"Me too. Especially not one of *those* girls. Look at the shirts they have on today," I said.

For some reason Marla and Jessie like to dress alike. It makes me sick. They call each other up and discuss what they're going to wear the next day so that they can match. This particular day, they were wearing white jeans and pink T-shirts that said GIRLS RULE across the front.

"Boy, what I'd give for a marker right now," said Fink. "I'd go over there and change those shirts so they said GIRLS DROOL."

"Hey, Fink," I said, "what are you wearing to school tomorrow?"

Fink looked at me funny.

"Why do you want to know?" he asked.

"So I can make sure *not* to wear the same thing," I said.

The bell rang and we went inside.

Fink and I have been in the same class every year but one since kindergarten. At the beginning of the year, it always takes the teacher a little while to get used to the fact that not only are we best friends, but we also have the same name. Not the same first name, and not the same last name, either. It's more complicated than that. Fink's first name is Boyd and my last name is Boyd. Boyd Fink and Nat Boyd. Pretty cool, right?

"As you know, class, we leave for Camp Willomet bright and early next Monday morning," Mrs. West began. "Buses will pick us up in the back parking lot at eight a.m. sharp. Please remember to pack a snack, since we'll be on the bus for about three hours and we will not be stopping except for emergencies."

Mad Dog made a rude noise and everybody laughed except Mrs. West, who scowled at him and went on.

"There are still a few permission slips that have not been turned in. You know who you are, so please get those to me as soon as possible," she said.

"Did you turn yours in?" I asked Fink.

He nodded.

"Me too," I said.

"This morning we'll be going to the auditorium to hear a presentation about the camp," Mrs. West continued. "Our guest speaker will be Mr. Volmer, the director from Camp Willomet, and I expect you to be on your best behavior."

She looked directly at Mad Dog when she said that.

"He will be presenting a slide show, followed by a question-and-answer session. If you have any questions or concerns about the camp, this will be your opportunity to bring them up," she said. "Please line up now in an orderly fashion and we'll proceed to the auditorium."

The slides the camp guy showed were old. You could tell because the kids had goofy haircuts, weird glasses, and clothes that no one would be caught dead wearing these days. We saw a lot of pictures of dorky looking kids with butterfly nets and dorky looking kids looking into microscopes and dorky looking kids wading in ponds catching slimy stuff. Then there were pictures of dorky looking kids sitting around campfires, toasting marshmallows and singing songs. But even though they all looked dorky, everybody seemed to be having a good time, and the place looked pretty nice, too, especially the cabins. They were little wooden houses with green doors and window frames, and inside each one there were six sets of metal bunk beds, each with a sleeping bag and a pillow laid out neatly on top of it.

"We're definitely going to share a bunk," whispered Fink. "You want the top or the bottom?"

"We could trade off, one night on top, the next night on the bottom," I whispered back.

"Cool," said Fink, giving me a thumbs-up.

Then Mr. Volmer showed us a slide of a big wooden tower.

"This is Mount Wood," he announced proudly. "Many campers say that it's their favorite thing at Camp Willomet. It's thirty-five feet tall. You'll all be given an opportunity to scale Mount Wood using ropes and harnesses. For the more daring among you, there is also a special bungee harness, which allows you to jump off after you've reached the summit. As you can see in the picture, there will be plenty of foam-rubber padding waiting for you at the bottom to cushion your landing. Every year we have a contest to see who can get up and back down the fastest. The winners' names are all engraved on a bronze plaque on the side of the tower."

There was a murmur of excitement in the auditorium.

"Are you going to jump?" I asked Fink.

"Not if my mother hears about it. That would go right on the top of the list for sure," said Fink, pretending to write with his finger in the air — "N-O T-O-W-E-R-S."

Camp Willomet was looking pretty good if you asked me — five days of fun stuff to do. Climbing Mount Wood would be awesome, and so would toasting marshmallows. My mother hardly ever lets me have sweets, especially sticky ones like marshmallows. But she wouldn't be there at camp with me, so I was definitely planning to enjoy a marshmallow or two.

Even the educational stuff about camp looked like fun. Science is one of my favorite subjects in school, especially when it has to do with animals. I love animals, but I only have one pet at home, a goldfish named Hercules. He's fine for a fish, but all he does is swim and eat and mess up his bowl. I'd like to have a dog or a cat, or even both, but my mom is allergic to fur. When she first told me that, I didn't believe her. I thought she was just saying it so we didn't have to get a pet. So Fink and I snuck his cat, Picklepuss, into our house to test her.

We hid Picklepuss in my room, and the minute my mom came home, I knew she'd been telling the truth. She started sneezing like crazy and she couldn't stop. Fink hid Picklepuss under his shirt and went home, and I ran the vacuum cleaner around my room for about an hour trying to get rid of every bit of fur he might have left behind. I felt terrible every time my mom sneezed, but at least she was happy about me vacuuming my room.

Besides Hercules, I have a bunch of tadpoles I ordered through the mail that are going to turn into frogs someday soon — but I don't count those as pets because as soon as they have legs I'm going to let them go. My mom's not allergic to frogs, but I don't think she'd like having twenty of them jumping around the house.

I'm thinking about getting a turtle after the tadpoles go. Or possibly newts. What I'd really like to have is some sort of a pet without fur that could learn tricks, but so far I haven't been able to find anything like that. I've never heard of a newt that rolls over or shakes hands, but who knows? Maybe that's just because nobody's tried hard enough to teach them.

After the slide show Mr. Volmer, the camp guy, asked us if we had any questions. Of course, Jessie Kornblume's hand was the first one up. Jessie loves to hear herself talk. She thinks she's smarter than everyone else because she got a 99.9 on the Farnsworth Aptitude test in fourth grade. Big deal! She doesn't seem that smart to me. The test was all multiple choice questions, anyway. She probably just got lucky.

"How do you plan to prevent the boys from raiding the girls' cabins at night?" Jessie asked.

Fink groaned.

"What makes you think anyone would be interested in coming to *your* cabin?" he said.

Jessie shot him a mean look, and Marla stuck her tongue out at him.

Mr. Volmer told Jessie that every day at Camp

Willomet we'd be getting up at the crack of dawn, and that by the time the end of the day rolled around, he was sure no one would have the energy to be playing any pranks.

Fink raised his hand.

"Will there be anything involving bats, balls, paddles, pucks, sticks, or rackets?" he asked.

Mr. Volmer looked confused.

"He means sports," I said.

"Oh, I see. There are no organized sports at Camp Willomet. Baseballs and mitts are optional. If you'd like to bring them along, feel free," said Mr. Volmer.

"See, I told you not to worry," I said to Fink.

There were a few more questions, and then we lined up and went back to class. Jessie and Marla were walking in front of us, chattering like crazy.

"They're probably planning their wardrobes for the trip," Fink said.

"Hey, maybe they could wear matching bear suits and get trapped and carted off to the zoo," I said. "Wouldn't that be great?"

"Yeah, or maybe we could tie antlers on their

heads and see if —" but Fink didn't finish his sentence. Instead he stopped and pointed at my leg.

"You're scratching," he said.

He was right. I was scratching my knee.

"Uh-oh," I said.

In case I haven't told you already, I have this weird thing with my knee. Whenever something bad is about to happen, it gets itchy. I quickly looked around to see if something dangerous was coming my way. Nothing was behind me and I didn't see anything out of the ordinary in any other direction, either.

"Maybe it's a false alarm," I said. "Sometimes I get itchy just because I'm itchy."

"Yeah," said Fink, "maybe it's nothing."

Sometimes it's just an innocent itch, a bug bite, or a loose thread tickling me. Unfortunately, this was not one of those times. Something bad was coming all right, something *really* bad.

CHAPTER TWO

"A or B?" I said to Fink on the way home from school later that day.

"Go ahead, lay it on me, Nat-Man," said Fink.

"Okay," I said, "A: you tell Jessie you want to sit next to her on the bus and hold her hand all the way to Camp Willomet, or B: you ask Marla where she got her GIRLS RULE T-shirt and tell her you think it's cool and you want to get one, too, so you can be triplets with Jessie and her."

"How long did Mrs. West say the ride to Camp Willomet would take?" Fink asked.

"Three hours," I told him.

"Too long to plug my nose, so I'll take B. You said

I had to ask her where she got the shirt and tell her that I want one, but you never said I actually had to get one and wear it," he said.

"Wait, let me give you a different one. That was way too easy," I said.

"No way!" cried Fink. "You know the rules. No changes. No re-dos. My turn."

A or B is a game Fink and I invented. It's one of our favorites. One person thinks up two creepy or gross or revolting things, and then the other person has to choose which one of the things he would rather do if he *had* to do one. We never actually make each other do the things, but the rule is: no matter how hard it is to choose, you have to pick one.

"Fine," I said, folding my arms across my chest, "but to make it fair you have to give me easy ones, like I gave you."

"Didn't anybody ever tell you life isn't fair?" Fink said. "Your mother must have some expression for that, right?"

My mother is the queen of expressions. She's got one for every situation and they're all really corny.

The worst part is that I'm so used to hearing them that sometimes I say them myself without even realizing it.

"I can't think of any about fairness, but she did tell me at dinner last night that there's more than one way to skin a cat," I told him.

"Wow, does she really hate cats that much?" asked Fink. "Remind me never to bring Picklepuss over to your house again."

"It's just an expression," I said. "It's not like she'd hurt your cat or anything, Fink. She's allergic, but she's not nuts."

"If you say so," said Fink, "but I'm still not bringing Picklepuss over again."

"Whatever. Give me my A or B already," I said.

"Okay, A: you eat a whole jar of mayonnaise, or B: you share a bunk at camp with Mad Dog instead of me."

Fink knows how much I hate mayonnaise. I just don't understand how people can put that stuff in their mouths. It ruins everything it touches, especially ham and cheese sandwiches. My mother once told me that some people dip french fries in it instead of ketchup. Boy, I hope I don't ever have to see that! When I'm old enough to have a car, I'm going to put a bumper sticker on it that says, SAY NO TO MAYO!

Fink also knows that I'm terrified of Mad Dog. Or at least I used to be. It's kind of a long story. See, Mad Dog's real name is Douglas Ditmeyer, and he's bad news. First of all he's big for his age. No, make that HUGE for his age. Second of all, he's got a temper and a mean streak about a mile wide. For a long time I managed to steer clear of him, and he pretty much left me alone, but all that changed when he found out that he needed braces.

My mom is Dr. Holly Boyd, the most popular orthodontist in town. She puts braces on everybody in Jeffersonville who needs them, so of course, Mrs. Ditmeyer brought her precious son Douglas to my mother to have his teeth straightened. The problem was, Mad Dog has this fear of dentists. And like everything about Mad Dog, from his feet to his temper, this fear was BIG.

The first time he came to see my mother, he cried

in her office and then he fainted. That is definitely unusual behavior for Mad Dog. I've seen him sneer, I've heard him growl, I've seen him give a hundred atomic wedgies, but I've never seen him cry.

Anyway, Mad Dog figured my mom would tell me what happened in her office, and that I'd blab it all over school, so he tried to scare me into keeping quiet. He did a pretty good job of it, too, which is why I had to buy that Manly Mint deodorant I was talking about before. When I get scared, sometimes I sweat, and sweating gives me B.O. No matter how much Manly Mint I used, Mad Dog could still manage to make me stink. Fortunately, though, I haven't had to use it in a while, not since Mad Dog and I made our deal.

Fink is the only one who knows that I've been afraid of Mad Dog ever since he swiped a used mousetrap off the custodian's cart and stuffed it, dead mouse and all, into somebody's gym shoe. But Jessie Kornblume overheard me say something about being scared of Mad Dog recently, and all of a sudden life got very complicated.

Girls are not like boys. They're much meaner, and when it comes to teasing, they are definitely better at it than us. I'm not saying that boys don't know how to tease, but girls are sneakier about it. They don't just go for the obvious, they dig around looking for embarrassing things about you that you really don't want anybody to know, and then they tease you about those things in front of everybody until you wish you could move to another planet.

So I'm sure you can understand why I wouldn't want Jessie and Marla to know that I'm afraid of Mad Dog. There's nothing they'd like better than a chance to sink their teeth into something juicy like that. But once I found out about Mad Dog's secret fear of dentists, I decided to strike while the iron was hot (one of my mom's corny expressions), and come up with a deal. I'd keep his secret if he kept mine. I wouldn't tell anybody — other than Fink, since like all best friends, Fink and I tell each other everything — if he would help me convince Jessie and Marla that he and I were good friends.

The first thing we did was fake a sleepover, which

was Fink's idea. How could they think I was afraid of Mad Dog if I was letting him sleep at my house? Of course, Mad Dog didn't really sleep over, we just made sure Jessie and Marla *thought* he had. It worked like a charm. They also think we've gone fishing and bowling together and that we're planning to build a clubhouse in my backyard. Fat chance.

"So what's your answer, A or B?" Fink asked me.

"I'll take B," I said. "If I ate a whole jar of mayonnaise, even if it was a little jar, I would definitely puke. And besides, Mad Dog doesn't really bug me anymore, since we made that deal."

"Speaking of deals, what's the deal with him and his braces? Do you think your mom is ever going to put them on him?" Fink asked me as we rounded the corner and headed down our street.

I shrugged.

"I don't know," I said. "Considering that he faints at the sight of her, I kind of doubt it. I don't think you can put braces on an unconscious person."

"Can you imagine having to put your fingers in his mouth?" Fink asked.

We both shuddered at the same time.

"I'd be scared he might bite me," I said.

"Yeah, and a bite from Mad Dog would definitely require rabies shots, don't you think?" asked Fink. "Plus he's got really bad breath. You ever smell it?"

"Yeah, he could peel paint right off a wall with that breath of his," I said.

"Is that one of your mother's expressions?" Fink asked.

"Nope. One of mine," I answered.

We were in front of Fink's house.

"Do you mind if we go to your house today instead of mine?" he asked, nervously looking up toward the house. "If my mom sees me, she's gonna make me practice my clarinet because I have a lesson tomorrow."

"Fine with me, but remember, the only snacks at my house are the healthy kind," I said, "so no complaining."

Fink's mom won't let him play baseball but she lets him eat anything he wants. Cake, corn dogs, Cheetos, ice cream — you name it. If I didn't like sports so much, I might wish we could trade places.

"Granola bars are bad, but practicing the clarinet is even worse," Fink said. "Hurry up before she looks out the window and sees us!"

We ran toward my house.

"Last one there is a rotten egg," I said.

"Nuh-uh! Last one there is a mouthful of mayonnaise!" shouted Fink, which made me laugh so hard that he actually caught up to me. He might have beaten me, too, if he hadn't tripped over his untied shoelaces right before we reached my house.

My mom's office is attached to the house. It has a separate entrance off the front porch and a big painted sign with a giant smile on it that says BOYD ORTHODONTICS. As we ran up the front steps, laughing and out of breath, we looked in the office window and saw my mom in her white coat, bending over a patient who was lying back in the chair. Even though all I could see was the feet, I could tell the patient was a man because his big waffle-soled boots were hanging over the end of the chair. Most of my mom's patients are kids, of course, but she has a few grown-ups, too, and this guy looked way too big to be a kid.

"Look at the size of those feet," I said.

"Yeah, like where's the beanstalk, Jack?" said Fink.

My mom looked up from her work and waved to us. We waved back, went inside, and headed straight for the kitchen.

"Are you sure she doesn't have *anything* good to eat in here?" Fink asked as he pulled open the refrigerator and started rummaging through the shelves like a hungry bear.

"Cheese is good," I said, "and so are dill pickles."

"Yeah, but cookies are better," said Fink.

"Hey, I warned you, no complaining. If you're looking for cookies, go home," I told him. "There are no cookies in there — trust me, none."

Fink took out the jar of pickles and handed it to me.

"I guess these will have to do. Fish me out a nice fat one, will you?" he asked.

While I got busy trying to open the jar of pickles, Fink stared at his reflection in the side of the toaster.

He kept licking the palm of his hand and using it to try to flatten down his hair, which was sticking up a little on the top of his head. Getting the pickle jar open was not easy. I tried brute strength first, but when that didn't work I smacked the bottom of the jar a few times and then banged on the lid with a big spoon. Finally, it popped open.

"Got it!" I said. "Ready for a fat one?"

But when I looked up, Fink had turned away from the toaster and was staring at me with a funny look on his face.

"What's the matter?" I asked. "Don't you want a pickle anymore?"

"Forget about the pickle. Look at my tongue. Does it look weird to you?" he asked.

"Weird how?" I asked.

"Weird like this," he said, sticking out his tongue for me to see.

He was right, it did look kind of strange. Blotchy.

"Does it hurt?" I asked.

"Not really," he said. "But my throat feels a little funny."

"Want me to look at it?" I asked.

"Sure," he said, opening his mouth.

"I can't see," I told him. "Let me get the flashlight and a knife."

"A knife?" he said. "You're not planning to cut my tongue off or something, are you?"

I went and pulled a butter knife out of the silverware drawer. Then I got the flashlight out from under the laundry room sink, where we keep it in case the electricity ever goes out.

"Calm down, Fink. My mom always pushes my tongue down with a knife when she wants to look at my throat," I told him. "It's not a sharp one, just a butter knife. See?" I held up the knife.

"Aren't you supposed to use one of those little wooden sticks like the doctor uses?" he asked nervously.

"A tongue depressor, you mean?" I said.

"Yeah, a tongue depressor," he said. "Why don't you use one of those instead of a knife?"

"Why? Because this is a kitchen, not a doctor's office, so I don't happen to have any tongue depressors lying around. What I've got is a butter knife, and if you want me to look at your throat, quit yappin' and open your mouth already, will you?" I said.

Fink opened his mouth and I pressed his blotchy tongue down with the knife and shone the flashlight on his throat.

"Whoa!" I said. "What are those weird-looking round things in the back of your throat?"

"Ohn thullth," he answered me, making an attempt to talk around the knife in his mouth.

"Tonsils? Is that what you said?" I asked him.

Fink nodded.

"They don't look like my tonsils. Mine are small and pink like little berries. Yours are big polka-dotted bowling balls."

"Wha?" Fink said, his eyes popping open wide. He pushed my hand away and took the butter knife out of his mouth.

"What do you mean, polka-dotted?" he said.

"Look for yourself, if you don't believe me," I said. "There's a mirror out in the hall."

Fink grabbed the flashlight and I followed him as

he ran into the front hall. He tipped his head back, and shining the light in his mouth, looked at his throat in the mirror. When he was finished, he turned off the flashlight and broke into a huge grin.

"How great is this?" he said.

"What are you talking about?" I said. "They look pretty gross to me, Fink."

"Yeah, but when my mom gets a load of these babies she's going to have to let me stay home from school tomorrow for sure. And if I don't go to school there's no way she's going to make me go to my clarinet lesson, either," he said. "No lesson, no practicing. It's a beautiful thing."

I followed him back into the kitchen.

"Aren't you worried at all about how big those things are? And about the polka dots?" I asked.

"Nah. Like I said, my throat doesn't hurt that much, only a little, so it can't be anything serious. Just serious enough to get me out of my clarinet lesson. Don't worry, I'll be back in school the day after tomorrow. Come on, let's go eat pickles in the tree," he said.

Fink grabbed a pickle out of the jar and headed out to the backyard to the old apple tree he and I like to climb up and hang out in.

I had just reached into the jar for my pickle when something made me stop and stand completely still. I waited until I was sure. Absolutely sure. My knee was itching again.

CHAPTER THREE

I decided not to tell Fink about my knee. I know I just said that we tell each other everything, and it's true. We do. But I wanted to wait a little while longer to make absolutely sure it was the real thing.

"I hope my parents don't find out about Mount Wood," Fink called down to me from up in the tree. "My mom's already uptight enough about me going away for five days."

I needed both hands to climb up the tree, so I stuck the pickle in my mouth and quickly scrambled up to where Fink was already sitting on a sturdy upper branch. Some pickle juice dripped down my chin and I wiped it off on my shirtsleeve.

"How'd you get up here so fast?" he asked. "What are you, part monkey or something? You don't have a tail you want to tell me about, do you?"

"Hey, you're the one who had that dream about having a tail, remember?" I said.

"Oh, yeah, I forgot about that," he said. "That was a weird one."

Fink and I have a lot of things in common besides having the same name. For instance, we both like strawberry ice cream, but not strawberries. We both like scary movies, especially the old black-and-white Alfred Hitchcock ones, and we both have a lot of weird dreams.

"So how did you get up here so fast, anyway?" Fink asked again. "I never saw you climb like that before."

"I don't know, maybe my arms are stronger from lifting all those heavy boxes for my mom last weekend when she was cleaning out the garage. But if you think that was fast, just wait 'til you see me climb Mount Wood," I said, brushing off my hands and taking a big bite of the sour pickle.

"Are you definitely going to climb it?" Fink asked.

"Definitely," I said. "Wouldn't it be cool to win the race and get your name engraved on that plaque for all time?"

"You want to know something?" Fink said. "Even if my mother doesn't find out about it, I'm not so sure I'm going to climb it. I don't really like high places. It makes me feel like I'm going to puke when I look down."

"We're up high right now," I said.

"Exactly, and you don't see me looking down, do you?" he said.

"Tell the truth, do you think I have any chance of winning that race?" I asked him. "Seriously, Fink. Do you think it could happen?"

"I guess so. But are you sure you want to do it? That foam rubber they have sitting at the bottom didn't look all that comfortable to me," Fink said.

"I bet a lot of people will try climbing it," I said.

"Well, if you're serious about wanting to win the race, you're going to have to practice," said Fink.

"How am I going to do that?" I asked. "I haven't seen any giant wooden towers around here to practice climbing up, have you?"

"You don't need to practice climbing, you're already good at that," said Fink. "It's the coming down part you have to work on. You have to practice jumping off tall things. I'll be your coach. We can be a team — the 'Mount Woodsters.'"

"If you think all this talk about coaching me, and being the 'Mount Woodsters' and all that, is going to help convince me to jump out of this tree with a bungee cord attached to my back, you can forget about it," I said.

"I don't have any bungee cords," he said. "I was thinking maybe I'd just hold on to the back of your underwear, push you out of the tree, and see how far you got."

"Very funny," I said.

Fink and I sat in the tree, eating our pickles and talking about nature camp.

"I wish the girls weren't coming," he said.

"Me too," I agreed. "Especially the Red Devils. I'm sure they're going to make total pains of themselves as usual."

"Yeah, but at least we'll have our own cabin," Fink said. "Hopefully it'll be far away from theirs."

"I'm sort of glad Mr. Galluzzi is going to be our counselor. He's pretty cool," Fink said.

"Yeah, and I'm glad Mrs. West let us pick our science project partners ourselves this time. I hate it when she does the choosing," I said.

"Like when she put us with Jessie and Mad Dog for that Vasco da Gama project," Fink said.

"At least we got an A," I said.

Mrs. West had told us that we'd all be doing science projects while we were away at camp. Fink and I were going to be partners, of course.

"So what are we gonna do for our project?" I asked him.

"I don't care, as long as whatever we're doing is far away from wherever the mosquitoes are hanging out," he said.

"You know what might be cool?" I said. "Ants."

"Ants?" he said. "You mean those annoying little things that crawl all over the counter if you leave any crumbs lying around? What's cool about them?"

"Lots. I saw this thing on TV all about ants a few weeks ago and they're really amazing. Did you know that some ants can lift things that are fifty times their own weight? If a person could do that it would mean they could lift a car."

"Really?" said Fink. "I'll bet it would take four to lift a Hummer, though. Those things are like tanks."

"And there's this kind of ant called a parasol ant that makes these underground gardens out of leaves they cut up, and then they grow mushrooms in the garden for food," I said.

"I hate mushrooms," said Fink.

"That's not the point. The point is, studying ants would be a cool project, don't you think?" I asked.

"What are we going to do, crawl around camp on our hands and knees looking for ants? What if there aren't any?" Fink asked.

"There will be," I said. "There are over twelve thousand species of them. Ants are everywhere. Look! There's one crawling on your hand right now."

Fink gently flicked the black ant off of his hand and we both watched it scurry away, waving its antennae nervously as it went.

"Okay, I'm sold. Why don't we go to the library tomorrow at school and see if they have any good ant books? We should find out what kind of ants live around the area where Camp Willomet is, so we don't waste time looking for those parasol guys if they only live in Madagascar or something," Fink said.

"We can't go to the library together at school tomorrow," I said.

"Why not?" asked Fink.

"'Cause you're not going to school tomorrow, remember?" I said. "You've got polka-dotted bowling balls living in your throat."

Fink swallowed and rubbed his throat with one hand.

"Oh, yeah," he said. "I forgot."

Fink and I hung out up in the tree for a little while

longer, but then he said that his throat was actually starting to hurt a little bit more, so he decided to go home.

I walked him to the door and at the exact same time he reached for the knob to turn it, my mom turned the knob from the outside and came in. They almost ran into each other.

"Oh, you startled me!" she said.

She was still wearing her white coat and she had a piece of gauze wrapped around her right hand.

"What happened to your hand?" I asked her.

"Occupational hazard," she said. "'Scuse me a sec while I grab some ice."

"What does 'occupational hazard' mean?" Fink whispered to me.

"It means something bad that can happen to you because of the kind of work you do," I explained.

"Oh, like you could get frostbite on your tongue if you're a Popsicle salesman?" Fink said.

"If you're a really disgusting Popsicle salesman who licks all of his own Popsicles before he sells them, sure," I said.

My mom came back with a plastic bag filled with ice. She held up her pointer finger, which was red and a little swollen.

"Ever hear the expression, 'Barking dogs seldom bite'?" she asked. "Well, when it comes to your friend Douglas Ditmeyer, it's not true."

"What are you talking about?" I asked.

"Douglas bit me," she said.

"He *did*?" I said. Suddenly, I remembered the big feet sticking off the end of my mom's chair. I told you he's huge for his age. The waffle-soled boots hadn't belonged to some grown-up, they'd belonged to Mad Dog!

"It was an accident," she said. "He really didn't mean to."

"Mad Dog *bit* you?" I said, still unable to believe what she'd said.

"Do you want me to call my mom?" Fink offered. "I'm sure she'd be glad to drive you over to the emergency room if you need to get shots or something."

He wasn't kidding, but my mom laughed anyway.

"That's sweet, Boyd, but it's no big deal. He didn't

break the skin. I'll be fine. Besides, every cloud has a silver lining. This bite is a symbol of success," she said, holding up the finger again.

"What success?" I asked.

"I finally got Douglas into his braces. It took some doing, let me tell you — but in the end I conquered his mouth, and more importantly he conquered his fear. Other than the bite, which as I said was an accident, he was as calm as can be. I don't think he's going to have any more trouble with dentists. Isn't that wonderful?"

Wonderful? Was she kidding? I looked at Fink. I could tell from the look on his face that he understood. If Mad Dog wasn't afraid of dentists anymore, that meant the deal I'd made with him was off. He could do or say anything he wanted now. I had nothing to hold over his head anymore. Fink didn't even bother to point out that I'd started scratching my knee again. We both knew why. I was doomed. Totally doomed.

CHAPTER FOUR

That night I had one of my dreams. I read some-
where that everyone has hundreds of dreams every
night, but I doubt that many people have the kinds of
dreams I do. Even Fink's aren't quite as extreme as
mine. Mine always seem to be either really weird or
really embarrassing, or sometimes both of those
things mixed together, which is the worst. This was
one of the mixed-together kind.

I was climbing a big tree while Fink stood at the
bottom with a stopwatch in his hand, telling me to
climb faster. I was climbing like crazy, when suddenly,
I realized that it wasn't a tree I was climbing at all. It
was a leg. Mad Dog's leg! He was a huge giant, with

legs as big as tree trunks and when he looked down at me, climbing up his huge pink leg like that, he opened his mouth and started laughing this horrible, mean laugh and I, of course, broke into a sweat. In case you're wondering if a person can have B.O. in a dream, the answer is yes.

Anyway, instead of regular braces, Mad Dog's mouth was full of barbed wire, all sharp and shiny and wrapped around his big yellow teeth. I could tell from the way he was looking at me and drooling, that he was planning to eat me. I wanted to get away and I knew the fastest way would be to jump, so I got up my nerve and threw myself off of Mad Dog's giant pink leg. But just as I jumped, he reached out and got ahold of the back of my underwear (I had Fink to thank for planting *that* idea in my head), and when I jumped off, the elastic made me spring right back up like a yo-yo. Talk about an atomic wedgie! This was the wedgiest ever. *Boing! Boing!* He kept doing it and doing it, until finally the elastic broke — *Twang!* — and I went flying through the air. I covered my eyes and screamed, "Catch me, Fink!"

41

And he did. Or at least I thought he did, until I opened my eyes and saw that it wasn't Fink who had caught me. It was Jessie Kornblume.

"P.U., Nat Boyd. You stink!" she said.

And that's when I woke up.

Okay, to be honest, there is one little detail that I left out. I guess because it's so embarrassing. But since I told you the rest of it, I might as well tell you the embarrassing part, too. Jessie was wearing a big white poofy wedding dress. It's not the first time, either. Whenever Jessie's in my dreams, she always shows up wearing that ridiculous dress. I can't stand Jessie Kornblume, so I wish I could figure out why she's in my dreams all the time. And don't ask me why she's always wearing that wedding dress, because I have no idea. All I know is that if she ever found out about it, I'd die.

I lay in my bed in the dark for a while, trying to get the images of Jessie in the poofy wedding dress and Mad Dog's mouth full of barbed wire out of my head. I looked over at the clock and saw that it was only five o'clock — another two hours until I had to get up for school — but I was afraid to go back to sleep in case the dream picked up where it had left off.

I decided to get up and go downstairs to the den, where the computer is. I hadn't checked my e-mail in a few days and I thought maybe I'd go online and see what I could find out about ants.

I didn't have any e-mails except for some junk mail from the company I bought my tadpoles from, but I did find an ant Web site that had some pretty interesting stuff on it. One thing that caught my attention was a whole section on ant behavior. Among other things, it said that ants warn other ants when there is danger present by releasing a strong smell. I was sort of happy to find out that I'm not the only one in the world who stinks when he's afraid.

I wrote down a few other cool ant facts to tell Fink about later, and then after a while I went back upstairs to see if maybe I could fall back to sleep. It worked, and an hour later when my alarm went off, I was sound asleep in the middle of another weird dream about an army of ants wearing tiny little party hats. This time, though, I'm happy to say, Jessie and her poofy wedding dress were nowhere in sight.

The next morning, Fink wasn't waiting on the corner for me the way he usually was at eight o'clock. So I figured he must have showed those tonsils to his mother and just like he predicted she would, she'd kept him home. I knew he was happy about not having to go to his clarinet lesson, but I was sorry he wasn't coming to school. I'm so used to being with Fink that it just doesn't feel right when he's not around.

I took our regular route and when I got to school the first people I ran into were Marla and Jessie. They were standing over by the bike racks and, as usual, they were dressed alike. I wished Fink was there. I knew he would have had something funny to say about what they had on. Jessie saw me standing there alone and came over.

"What science project are you and Fink going to do?" she asked.

I shrugged. "Why do you care?" I asked her.

"I don't, really. I was just wondering," she said.

By then Marla had come over and joined us.

"We're not sure what we're doing for the project yet," I lied. I wasn't about to tell the Red Devils we were doing ants. They might try to steal our idea.

"What are you doing?" I asked.

"We're going to count tree rings so we can tell how old the trees are at the camp," Marla said as though it was the most brilliant thing in the world.

"It was my idea," said Jessie proudly. "It's a fascinating scientific phenomenon."

Jessie is eleven, just like all the rest of us, but she talks like she's a teacher or something. She might know a lot of big words, but even an idiot can tell you that ants are a million times more interesting than tree rings.

"Not that I actually care or anything, but where's Fink?" asked Jessie, looking around.

"He's home sick," I told her.

"What's he got?" Marla asked, leaning toward me and turning her ear in my direction like I was about to tell her some deep dark secret.

"Big tonsils," I said, loudly in her ear.

Marla jumped back, rubbing her ear and scowling at me.

"You mean *tonsillitis*?" Jessie asked.

Another one of those fancy words. She's such a show-off it makes me sick.

"It's no big deal, just a sore throat," I said. "I'm sure he'll be fine by tomorrow."

"Maybe," said Jessie, "and maybe not."

"What do you mean?" I asked.

"If he has tonsillitis, he might have to get his tonsils taken out," she said. "That's what happened to my cousin."

"Really?" I said.

"Yeah, and he said it hurt like crazy, too," she said.

"How long did it take?" I asked.

"What? The operation?"

"No, I mean how long was he sick?"

"I think he missed two weeks of school," she told me.

Two weeks? Nature camp was five days away.

"Hey, Nat, where are you going?" Jessie called after me as I ran toward the front door. "The bell didn't even ring yet."

But I didn't stop to answer her. I was in too big a hurry to get inside. I had to call Fink and see how he was feeling.

Fink's mother answered the phone.

"Hi, Mrs. Fink. I was wondering if I could speak to Fink — I mean, Boyd — for a minute," I said, still a little out of breath from my run.

"Oh, hi, Nat. Boyd's sleeping right now. He had kind of a rough night, poor thing. His fever went up to 103. Why don't you give him a call a little later, after you get home from school, okay? He should be up by then."

"Oh, sure. Okay. Tell him I hope he feels better," I said.

"I will," she said. Then she hung up.

I stood there with the phone in my hand for a long time. The bell rang, and kids streamed in, heading for their classrooms. Marla and Jessie walked past.

"What's the matter with you?" Jessie asked. "You look like you just saw a ghost."

I'd just seen something, all right, but it wasn't a ghost. It was a glimpse of my future — and I did not like the way it looked at all.

"You better hurry up or you're going to get marked late," Marla said to me as she and Jessie headed on toward the classroom. Then she added over her shoulder, "Not that I care."

But being late to class was the least of my worries. Could Fink really have tonsillitis? No, it just couldn't be true, I told myself as I reached down and absentmindedly scratched my knee. That would be too awful.

CHAPTER FIVE

"Mr. Boyd?" said Mrs. West. "Where is your shadow this morning?"

Mrs. West always calls us "mister" and "miss" when she calls on us in class.

"He's sick," I said.

"With *tonsillitis*," Jessie chimed in.

"He does NOT have tonsillitis!" I yelled.

"Mr. Boyd, there's no need for you to raise your voice in my classroom that way," Mrs. West said sternly.

"Well, she doesn't know what she's talking about. All Fink has is a sore throat. He'll be fine," I said. "He told me so himself."

I sort of surprised myself with how angry I'd gotten all of a sudden. I can't even remember the last time I yelled in class. Just because Jessie said something didn't mean it was so. In fact, most of the time I don't listen to anything she says at all, because she's wrong about so many things.

"It's really nothing," I told Mrs. West again, more calmly this time. "He'll be fine."

"Let's hope you're right," said Mrs. West. "It would certainly be a shame if he was too ill to go to camp next week."

When she said that, instead of getting angry, I suddenly felt worried. But then I kept telling myself that Fink was going to be fine. He was probably just milking this sore throat thing for all it was worth to make sure that he wouldn't have to go to his clarinet lesson. Yeah, his mom said he had a fever, but Fink's pretty clever. Maybe he found a way to make the thermometer go up or something. I think you can do that with a lightbulb. He said that he'd be back in school by the next day and I was sure he would be. I refused to worry.

Still, I couldn't seem to concentrate on anything all morning. After lunch, I went to the school library and took out a book about ants, but it turned out to be a bad one. The whole thing was told from the ant's point of view as though it was writing a journal. It felt more like a story for little kids than a science book. The ant kept saying things like "Yum, yum! Aphids sure taste good!" and "It's an honor to be asked to clean up the droppings of the queen, Your Highness." I gave up after a few pages and put it away.

I kept thinking about Fink. What if Jessie was right and he had tonsillitis? What if he had to have an operation? And what if on Monday — no, I wasn't even going to let myself go there. Fink wasn't sick. He just didn't want to go to his clarinet lesson, that's all.

I tried to read some more of the ant book, but it was just too annoying. Finally I asked Mrs. West if I could go back to the library to do some more re-search. She gladly let me go.

"I'm pleased to see you taking such an interest in your science project already, Mr. Boyd," she said as she handed me the hall pass. I felt a little guilty. The truth was, I wasn't planning to do any more research for my science project. I wanted to see what I could find out about tonsillitis. I was almost positive Fink didn't have it, but I just wanted to make sure.

I looked up "tonsils" in the library computer system. Then I went and pulled a couple of books off the shelf. I had just learned that tonsils are like filters, which keep germs from settling in our throats and causing infections, when I felt a warm breath on the back of my neck. And this particular breath didn't smell very good. I knew who it was right away.

"Uh, hi, Mad Dog, what's up?" I said, turning around and hoping that my voice didn't sound as scared as I was.

"What's up is this," he said, and he bared his teeth at me.

The metallic shine was so bright it made me blink.

"Wow, those braces look, um, really cool, Mad Dog," I said. "Very shiny."

"Yeah? Well, they hurt," he said.

"My mom says that's usually how it is in the beginning. You gotta put that wax she gives you on the wires for the first few days until your mouth gets used to having all that metal in there," I said. "I wouldn't know firsthand, because as you can see I don't have braces myself — not yet, anyway — but I've heard her telling her patients that the first few days are the hardest. She says — no pain, no gain."

I knew I was talking too much, but he wasn't saying anything and somebody had to fill the uncomfortable empty space between us.

"They hurt," he said, baring his teeth at me again. "And I don't like it when things hurt me."

I felt a warm trickle of sweat roll down my ribs.

"Me neither," I said, "but like I said, my mom always tells her patients that they gotta use that wax she gives —"

"When somebody hurts me, I hurt them back," he said, interrupting me.

My mom had told me that Mad Dog had bitten her by accident. Was that wrong? Had he bitten her to pay her back for putting on the braces?

"In case you're wondering," said Mad Dog, "I didn't mean to bite your mom."

Okay, that was a little scary. Was Mad Dog reading my mind?

"I'm sure you didn't mean to," I said. "You wouldn't want to hurt your dentist."

"Nope. But I might want to hurt you," he said, flashing those big metal teeth at me again.

"Why would you want to do that?" I asked as another trickle of sweat rolled down my side.

He shrugged.

"My teeth hurt. I gotta take it out on somebody, don't I?" he said.

And just like that, my fate was sealed. From then on, no matter how crazy it sounded, no matter how illogical it was, I was going to be the one who paid the price for whatever discomfort my mother caused in Mad Dog's horrible-smelling mouth. No wonder my knee had been itching so much lately. Could things get any worse?

"Nat Boyd, you big liar! You told Mrs. West you

were coming here to do research," said an all-too-familiar voice from behind me.

Apparently things *could* get worse. Jessie was standing there with her hands on her hips, looking at the books that were all lying open on the table.

"I *am* doing research," I said quickly.

"Yeah, right. Are you trying to tell me that you and Fink are doing tonsils as your science project?" she asked. "What do I look like, an idiot?"

That was a setup if I've ever heard one. Fink never would have passed up an opportunity for the obvious comeback to that line, but I was too freaked-out at the moment to even think straight, let alone come up with an insult for Jessie.

Where was Fink when I needed him? I know he wanted to get out of his clarinet lesson, but this was serious. I needed him to protect me from Mad Dog *and* Jessie. I just wasn't any good without him. I looked at the clock and was happy to see there were only five minutes left until the dismissal bell.

"Hey, we better get back to class," I said, quickly

flipping the books closed and jamming them back on the shelf. Then I squeezed between two library tables in order to avoid having to pass either Mad Dog or Jessie to get to the door. "Mrs. West will keep us after school if we're not there when the bell rings."

As I hurried down the hall to the classroom, one of my mother's expressions suddenly popped into my head — "Where there's smoke, there's fire." It means that if it seems like there's going to be trouble, there probably *is* going to be trouble. I didn't know it yet, but that expression fit my situation perfectly.

CHAPTER SIX

After school, I stopped at the Bee Hive snack bar to pick up something to bring to Fink. He loves the Bee Hive, but when we go there I usually only get water, because my mom won't give me money for sweet snacks.

"What'll it be?" the guy behind the counter asked me.

"An apple a day keeps the doctor away," I said.

I slapped my forehead. Why do I have to have a mother who makes me say things like that? It's so embarrassing.

"Uh, a large apple juice, please," I said.

"Small is kiddie, large is really medium, super is a

large, and super-duper is the biggest," he told me. "You still want a large?"

Why do people have to make life more complicated than it already is?

"Give me a super-duper apple juice, please," I said, "with a lid." I used my own money to buy the juice.

Even though my mother's expressions drive me crazy, a lot of times they're true. I hoped that the juice would keep the doctor away and speed up Fink's recovery somehow, too.

"It's just a little sore throat," I told myself, "no big deal."

I rang Fink's bell and his mom answered the door, but she didn't ask me in, the way she usually does.

"Hey, Mrs. Fink," I said. "I just wanted to check on Boyd and bring him some juice. I want to make sure he's one hundred percent okay by Monday."

"Monday?" she asked.

"Yeah, that's when we leave for Camp Willomet," I reminded her.

"Oh, I'm afraid camp is out of the question for Boyd, Nat," she said, shaking her head.

I knew that look. The overprotective look. I'd seen it a million times when she was telling Fink he couldn't do something because it wasn't safe. And I knew exactly what the problem was, too: Mount Wood. Somehow she must have found out about it. Maybe Fink blabbed it, or maybe she heard about it from another parent, but somehow she'd found out about it.

"If it's about Mount Wood, Mrs. Fink, I promise I won't let him . . ." I said, holding my hand over my heart like I was swearing to tell the truth. "I *promise*. In fact, I won't even climb it myself if that'll make you feel better. We'll do arts and crafts, and make some more key chains or something. Please! Fink has to come to nature camp. We're partners. We're doing ants."

"I'm sorry, Nat, but I'm afraid he can't go," she said again.

I was getting nowhere with this on my own. Maybe if Fink and I worked on her together we could get her to give in.

"Can I see him?" I asked as I started to go inside. She put her hand up to stop me.

"I'm sorry, Nat, but no. It's for your own good. The doctor says he's contagious," she told me. "I called your mother and told her to keep an eye on you, too, just in case he already infected you. Wouldn't that be a shame?"

"What's he got?" I asked, even though I had a sad feeling I already knew the answer.

"Tonsillitis," she said.

Tonsillitis. Jessie had been right.

"He doesn't have to have an operation, does he?" I asked.

"We won't know for a few days," she told me. "The doctor wants to see how he does with the antibiotic."

I took an antibiotic once for strep throat. I felt completely better in two days! Suddenly, I was hopeful.

"If the medicine works, do you think maybe he can still go to camp on Monday?" I asked.

"We'll see," she said. "It's too early to tell."

I gave Mrs. Fink the super-duper juice and told her to tell Fink to call me as soon as he could. Then I walked home.

"There's still hope," I told myself. "She said it herself. It's too early to tell."

Fink called later that afternoon and I could barely recognize his voice.

"You sound like a girl," I said.

"Thanks a lot," he said.

"Sorry, Fink. I didn't mean to insult you. You just don't sound like yourself is all I meant," I said.

"Don't worry about it. And thanks for the juice."

"Sure, no problem," I said. "Did it help?"

"Well, I'm not thirsty anymore, if that's what you mean, but my throat still hurts," he said. "It's not too bad, though. I just sound funny."

"Your mom said the doctor gave you antibiotics. Make sure you don't forget to take them, 'cause those things work really fast sometimes. I bet you're going to be fine by Monday," I said. "Don't you think?"

"Maybe. But you know, if you want me to come to Camp Willomet so bad, you really shouldn't have mentioned Mount Wood to my mom. She's been bugging me about it ever since you were here," he said.

"I'm really sorry. That was so *dumb*," I said.

61

"That's 'cause you're a *bum*," he answered.

"Give me a *break*," I said.

"Give me a *snake*," he said.

Fink made up this rhyming game a long time ago. It always starts the same way. Whenever I happen to say the word *dumb* at the end of a sentence, Fink starts rhyming and we just keep going until we run out of rhymes. I took it as a really good sign that he was feeling well enough to be playing it.

"You have to get *better*," I said.

"You big bed-*wetter*," he answered.

I laughed.

"That's a really good *rhyme*."

"I can do it every *time*," he said.

"Oh, yeah? Then why don't you have some *licorice*?" I said.

That's the quickest way to end the game because nothing rhymes with licorice. The closest we've ever been able to come is *ticklish* — but that's not a real rhyme. It only sort of sounds like a rhyme. Fink never seems to get tired of the game, but whenever I do, I toss that word in and it's all over. Even though I was glad Fink was playing, I wanted to stop the game because I had something important to talk to him about.

"I need some advice," I said.

"At your service, Natalie," he said.

Fink has a lot of nicknames for me: *Nat-Man, Nat-o*, and unfortunately, *Natalie*.

"I'm going to ignore that," I said, "because I really need your help."

I told him about Mad Dog and the "I have to take it out on somebody" thing.

"Maybe you should tell your mom," Fink said.

"Why would I do that?" I asked.

"I don't know, so maybe she can be really careful not to hurt him too much when she's working on his mouth," Fink said.

"It's not like she's hurting him on purpose, you know. Braces are just uncomfortable. But if he's going to hold me personally responsible for everything she does in his mouth, I'm in trouble. Have you ever really looked at Mad Dog's teeth?" I asked. "They're really bad."

"Crooked, you mean?" asked Fink.

"Big time crooked," I said. "It's gonna take years to straighten them out. *Years,* Fink. You understand how serious this is?"

Fink said he would think about it and try to come up with a brilliant solution to get Mad Dog off my back.

"Trust me. I'll think of something," he said.

I tried to get him to come up with at least part of an idea right then. I wanted to get started with the Mad Dog problem as soon as possible, but Fink said he had to get off the phone because all the talking was making his throat hurt more.

"You better get well soon, *or else,*" I told him before we hung up.

"Or else what?" he asked.

"I don't know, just *or else,* okay?" I said.

"That sounds like a threat, Nat-Man," said Fink.

"I just want to make sure you understand that I'm *never* going to forgive you if you don't recover by Monday. There's no way I'm going to Camp Willomet without you," I said.

"I'll do my best," said Fink.

The funny thing is, as sick as Fink was, there was somebody else in town who was even sicker than he was at that moment. Somebody with red hair and beady little eyes and a couple of giant, polka-dotted tonsils of her own.

CHAPTER SEVEN

Friday was not a good day. I didn't even bother to wait for Fink on the corner. I knew he wasn't coming to school. I'd called the night before, and his mom had said his throat was too sore for him to even come to the phone. I kicked a stone all the way to school, pretending that it was one of Fink's polka-dotted tonsils.

"You tell your friend Fink that I'm going to go over there and personally wring his neck for making Marla sick," Jessie said as soon as I set foot in the schoolyard that morning.

"What are you talking about?" I asked, giving the tonsil stone one last angry kick and sending it shooting across the yard toward the school, where it bounced off the brick wall. *Ping!*

"Marla is sick," Jessie said.

"So?" I said.

"So, she has tonsillitis," she said.

"She *does*?" I was shocked.

"Yes," said Jessie, "and I think you should know she's seriously thinking about having her father sue Fink."

Marla's father is a hotshot lawyer whose name is always in the papers because of some important case he's handling. Ever since I've known her, Marla has been telling people her father is going to sue them. All you have to do is look at her cross-eyed and she threatens to take you to court, but it's all hot air.

"Look, it's not Fink's fault Marla got tonsillitis. They don't hang out together. Fink can't stand her. She probably caught it from someone else. Or maybe *she* gave it to *him*. Did you ever think of that?" I asked.

"That's impossible. He was sick before she was," said Jessie, pushing up her glasses the way she always does when she thinks she's right about something.

"Yeah, well, for your information, Miss Smarty-pants, you can have it without knowing it and be contagious even though you don't feel sick yet yourself," I told her.

I'd read that in the tonsil book the day before in the library. Jessie looked at me and even though her glasses had slipped down her nose a little, she didn't push them back up. I guess for once I'd managed to impress her by telling her something she didn't already know.

The bell rang and we went inside. I put my lunch box in the closet and went to see if there were any homework sheets in the mailboxes by the door. I checked Fink's box first. Mrs. Fink hadn't been letting me go inside to give the homework to him myself, but I'd been bringing him his mail and work sheets every day since he'd gotten sick.

When I reached into my box, instead of the math sheet, there was something wet and cold in there. I yanked my hand out and found that my fingers were all red. At first I was scared. Had I cut myself? Was it blood? But then I caught a whiff of a familiar tomato smell and realized it was ketchup.

"Gotcha," said Mad Dog, slapping me hard on the back as he walked past me on the way to his seat. I wiped my hands with a tissue and took a clean math sheet from the pile of extras on the shelf. Then I went to sit down. It made me sad to look at Fink's empty desk, so I looked the other way as I walked past it to my own.

In class, Mrs. West made an announcement.

"Due to serious illness, I'm sorry to report that two of your classmates, Mr. Fink and Miss Dundee, may be unable to attend camp with us next week," she said. "We wish them both a speedy recovery, but just in case they are not able to join us, I would like to ask that Mr. Boyd and Miss Kornblume become science project partners in their absence."

"*What?*" Jessie and I both said at the same time.

"I'd like you to work together," she said.

Oh, great. Like it wasn't bad enough that Fink was sick, and Mad Dog was after me, now I needed to deal with *this*?

"But we can't work together. Marla and I chose our topic specifically to work on with each other,"

Jessie whined. "It's very scientific, Mrs. West. Nat probably wouldn't even be able to understand it."

"Ha! What's so hard to understand about tree rings?" I said. "They're boring. I understand that perfectly."

"Oh, yeah? Well, if your topic is so great, what is it, anyway?" asked Jessie.

"Ants," I said proudly.

"Ants?" snorted Jessie. "What's interesting about ants? Everybody hates them. They're pests, just like you and your contagious little friend, Fink."

"THAT'S ENOUGH!" said Mrs. West loudly. "I do NOT want to hear any more fuss about this. You two are partners. Is that understood?"

Jessie and I glared at each other, but neither of us said another word.

"I don't care which project you choose to work on — ants or tree rings — but I want you to work it out together and let me know on Monday what you've decided," she said. Then she picked up her chalk and started writing on the board. The discussion was over. It was a done deal. Corn Bloomers and I were science project partners whether we liked it or not.

It was a long day, but I made it through despite the fact that Jessie glared at me all day and Mad Dog growled at me every time I got within two feet of him.

After school I went straight home and called Fink. I still hadn't given up hope.

"Please tell me you're feeling better," I said as soon as he picked up the phone.

"Actually, I'm not," he said in his funny, croaky voice. "My throat still hurts and my temperature is back up to 102."

He did sound pretty bad. Suddenly I felt guilty for being so worried about my own problems. All that really mattered was that Fink was sick.

"Do you think you're going to have to have that operation?" I asked.

"They don't know yet. But the doctor called today and don't be mad, but he said I definitely can't go to camp," Fink told me.

My heart sank right down into my toes. Fink

wasn't coming to camp. Fink wasn't coming to camp. I had to say it a couple of times before I could even start to believe it was true.

"I'm sorry, Nat-o," Fink said.

"Hey, you don't have to apologize," I said quickly. "I'll be fine."

But Fink knows me too well to think I was really as okay with it as I was making it sound.

"Are you worried about the science project?" he asked. "Because I know you can handle the ant thing alone. You're the one who thought of it. You already know so much about them you could probably do the report right now, no problem."

"Yeah," I said. "Probably." I didn't have the heart to tell him that because he was sick, I was going to have to work with Jessie. I knew he'd feel bad about that.

"How was Mad Dog today?" Fink asked.

"Oh, he was fine," I said. "No problem at all."

There was silence on the other end of the phone.

"Knock it off," Fink finally said. "I can tell he did something. What was it? What did he do?"

"Nothing, really. He just misplaced his ketchup in my mailbox. But I have a feeling that was minor compared to the other things he plans to do," I said.

"I wonder what kinds of things he has planned," Fink said.

"I don't," I said. "Whatever they are, I'm sure they're bad."

"Don't worry. As soon as my fever goes down, I'll be able to think straight again. I'm sure I can come up with a way to get him to lay off," he said.

"Thanks," I said, but I knew by the time Fink was better it was going to be way too late.

I talked to Fink a few more times over the weekend. I kept hoping for a miracle. A sudden recovery that would amaze everyone. I pictured Fink jumping out of his bed feeling great, stuffing things in his duffel bag at the last minute and running to meet us at the bus on Monday morning. But Monday morning at 7:45, when my mom dropped me off in the parking lot with my sleeping bag and pillow and all the rest of my junk, the only person waiting for me was Mad Dog.

CHAPTER EIGHT

Fortunately I didn't have to sit by Mad Dog on the bus. I'm not sure I could have taken that for three hours. I had smeared on an extra layer of Manly Mint that morning just in case there was trouble, but Mad Dog ended up sitting with David Framer.

David and Mad Dog were science project partners, and when Mrs. West had suggested they work together, David hadn't looked exactly thrilled. But he hadn't made a stink about it, either. Maybe that's because he's the fastest runner in the whole fifth grade and he figured if Mad Dog gave him any trouble, he could outrun him if he had to. Or maybe it was because he'd noticed that the only person Mad

Dog seemed interested in making trouble for lately was me.

No sooner had I breathed a sigh of relief that I wasn't going to have to sit with Mad Dog, did I realize I was going to have to sit with Jessie. All the science project partners had to sit together. Ugh.

As Mrs. West called out names, we got on the bus in pairs. When she came to Jessie and me, she asked us what we had decided to do our science project on.

"We need a little more time," Jessie told her. "We haven't been able to come to an amicable decision yet."

Blah, blah, blah, enough with the big words already. Why didn't she just say that we hadn't been able to agree on anything because every time we tried to talk about it we just ended up fighting and calling each other names?

"By the time we arrive at camp I want the two of you to have made a decision," Mrs. West said. "I don't care which topic you choose, just as long as you decide on something to work on together."

We said okay, but I wasn't sure how we were going to do that. Personally, I had absolutely no intention of walking around in the woods with Jessie Kornblume, looking at stumps, and I'm sure she felt the same way about poking around in anthills with me.

Jessie and I got on the bus and headed toward the back where there were more empty seats. Mad Dog and David were sitting about halfway back, and as we walked past them, Mad Dog shot his foot out into the aisle and tripped me. As I fell, my foot accidentally caught on Jessie's leg and yanked her over, too, so that she fell right on top of me.

"Watch it, you clumsy oaf," she said.

"You watch it," I said. "You're squishing me."

Camp was off to a wonderful start.

Everyone was talking and singing and laughing and playing cards and all kinds of other fun stuff with their seatmates while the bus bumped along toward camp. And why shouldn't they all be having a ball? After all, they got to *choose* who they wanted to work with. Jessie and I sat there without saying anything for the first hour of the trip, until finally she broke the silence.

"I can't believe they're not here," she said.

76

"Who?" I asked.

"Who do you think? Marla and Fink," she said. "I can't believe they couldn't come. Marla and I have been talking about nature camp since second grade. And now we're never going to get to go together."

"Tell me about it. Fink and I have been talking about it since kindergarten," I said.

The bus was getting warm, so I stood up, took off my sweatshirt, and stuffed it into the little compartment above our seats.

"Hey, everybody," yelled a familiar voice from a few rows ahead of us, "get a load of the twins."

It was Mad Dog and he was pointing at me.

"What's he talking about?" Jessie asked me.

I looked down and realized to my horror that Jessie and I were both wearing red T-shirts.

"Aw, isn't that sweet?" said Mad Dog. "They match."

I groaned and sat back down.

"Did you have to wear a red T-shirt today?" I asked her as I slid down miserably in my seat.

"Did *you*?" she snapped back.

We sat without talking until she broke the silence again.

"What's wrong with tree rings, anyway?" she asked.

"They're just boring, is all," I said.

"That's only because you don't know anything about them," she said, pushing up her glasses. "They are actually a fascinating scientific —"

"Phenomenon," I finished the sentence for her. "Yeah, I know, but they're still boring."

"And ants aren't?" she said.

"No. They're not," I said.

"Okay. Tell me one interesting thing about ants," she said, then she pushed up her glasses and crossed her arms across her chest. "I'm waiting."

"Okay, every anthill holds a single family of ants and they all have the same mother, the queen. The queen's only job is to make ant babies and almost all the babies she makes are females. Those females are the worker ants. Then in the spring, a few male ants are born, but they don't work. They just hang out inside the hill waiting for the big day," I explained.

"What big day?" Jessie asked, and I could tell from the way she was leaning forward in her seat that she was getting sucked in by the story.

"The wedding day. See, the boy ants are born with wings, and so are a few special girl ants. They're called the princes and princesses. They mate, and then the girls fly off to become queens of their own hills."

"What happens to the boys?" Jessie asked.

"They die," I said.

"Cool," she said.

"Yeah, I thought you'd like that part," I said.

"Is there more?" Jessie asked.

"You mean, more interesting stuff about ants?" I asked.

"Yeah," she said.

"Tons more," I said.

She leaned back in her seat again and was quiet for a minute, like she was thinking about something. Then she sighed. "Okay, fine. We'll do ants," she said.

"Really?" I was surprised.

"Yes, I hate to admit it, but I think they might be more interesting than tree rings," she said.

"Really?" I asked again. I couldn't believe Jessie Kornblume was admitting that something I'd thought of was more interesting than something she'd thought of. She never would have done that if Marla had been around. I didn't have very long to enjoy my victory, though, because two seconds later, Mad Dog was standing by us, gearing up to make more trouble.

"How are you two little lovebirds doing?" he asked, with a big shiny metal smile.

Jessie rolled her eyes and I didn't say anything, hoping maybe he would just go away.

"Mr. Ditmeyer!" Mrs. West called from the front of the bus. "If you're on your way to the bathroom, please proceed. And if not, then kindly retake your seat."

Mad Dog gave me a last sneer and then went back to his seat.

"What's with him? Why is he being so mean to you all of a sudden?" Jessie asked. "I thought you guys were friends."

"*Friends?*" I said without thinking. "Me and Mad Dog?"

"Yeah, I mean, you have sleepovers and go bowling together, don't you?" she asked, giving me a funny look.

"Oh, yeah. Sometimes we do, sure. But lately he's just been kind of in a bad mood. It's nothing personal. I think maybe his braces are just making him grumpy or something," I said, trying to cover my mistake.

The last thing I needed right then was to have Jessie getting suspicious about me being afraid of Mad Dog. Like I said, girls can NOT be trusted with that kind of information.

At a little before eleven o'clock that morning, the bus pulled off the highway and we headed up a steep hill with thick, dark woods on either side of the road. We wound around and around on the narrow road until finally, just as I was beginning to feel a little queasy from all the turns, we saw the sign for Camp Willomet.

As we got off the bus, I kept my eye on Mad Dog, making sure not to give him another opportunity to trip me. We went and told Mrs. West that we had agreed on ants for our project and she smiled.

"Good job. I know it's hard for both of you that your best friends can't be here at camp with you," she told us. "But who knows? By the end of the week, you two may find that you have more in common than you ever could have imagined. You may even become friends. Stranger things have happened."

Really? I thought. Like what?

CHAPTER NINE

"Where's Mount Wood, anyway?" somebody asked.

I looked around. I didn't see anything that looked like the photo we'd seen of the tall tower. Even though I'd been spending most of my energy missing Fink and trying to stay out of Mad Dog's way since we'd left, Mount Wood had been in the back of my mind the whole time, too. I kept picturing my name engraved on that bronze plaque. I really wanted to win the race.

Mrs. West was busy getting all the girls lined up. Jessie had joined the line, dragging her duffel bag and carrying her sleeping bag under one arm. It was strange to see her standing there without Marla. I was just so used to seeing them together, it didn't look right somehow. I wondered if it looked the same way to see me standing around without Fink.

"Follow me, girls," Mrs. West was saying, "we're going to be staying in 'Evergreen,' which is one of the north cabins. Boys, your cabin is called 'Yucca.' It's on the south side, but please wait here for your chaperone. He was right behind us before. I'm sure he'll be here any minute."

"How come Mr. Galluzzi didn't come on the bus with us?" I asked Danny Lebson, who was standing next to me holding his junk. Danny is another one of my mother's patients, but unlike Mad Dog, he doesn't hold me responsible for his tinsel teeth.

Danny shrugged. "Beats me," he said.

Just then, a horn honked and we saw an old blue car, with a HONK IF YOU LIKE TO READ bumper sticker on it, pull up behind the bus. I heard several of the boys groan. We all knew who it was.

"It's Mootz," somebody said. "You don't think he brought those lousy puppets with him, do you?"

Something let out a low growl behind me and I

84

jumped, thinking it was a wild animal. It was Mad Dog. For a change, he wasn't directing his anger at me. He was growling at Mootz. I guess he wasn't happy to see him, either.

Mr. Mootz is a substitute teacher. He's about a hundred years old and whenever he fills in for a teacher who's sick or absent, he always brings these awful puppets along with him. Their names are Doozy and Dontsy. His wife made them out of a couple pairs of old socks. Mr. Mootz tells the same old stories with them every time he comes, and they weren't even good the first time around.

He hopped out of his car, wearing checkered shorts and long black socks with his brand-new, way-too-white sneakers. "Hello, boys!" he called, giving us a big wave.

"Where's Mr. Galluzzi?" Mad Dog asked.

"Mr. Galluzzi had a family emergency and wasn't able to be here, so guess who's come to camp out with you instead?" He reached into the backseat of the car and came out with a puppet on each hand. "It's your old pals Doozy and Dontsy!"

I won't bore you with the rest of his routine, but let's just say we all had to shake hands with the puppets before Mr. Mootz finally led us to our cabin on the south side of camp.

In the pictures we saw in the auditorium when Mr. Volmer came to show us slides of the camp, the cabins had been white with green doors and shutters, and they'd looked pretty nice and new. That's probably because they were nice and new *back then*. Now they were totally beat up, with peeling paint, and windows and doors that were so warped and crooked they didn't shut properly, making it very easy for things like mosquitoes, spiders, and flies to get in. The whole place smelled musty and damp and it fit my mood perfectly. Rotten.

"What a dump," said Mad Dog. For once we agreed. Whoever named our cabin "Yucca" should have named it "Yuck-o" instead.

"Every camper grab a bunk," said Mr. Mootz. Everyone scrambled to get a good bunk to share with a friend, but I just sat down on my duffel bag in the middle of the room, scratching my knee and waiting until everyone was finished. There were two bunks left, but one of them had no mattress so I had to take the other one. It was a top bunk, right next to the door, and guess who had the bottom bunk? Mad Dog, of course.

I tossed my sleeping bag and pillow up onto the bunk and was about to climb the ladder when Mad Dog reached out, grabbed my ankle, and held on tight.

"Where do you think you're going?" he growled. "This is a toll ladder. You have to pay me if you want to use it."

"Look, Mad Dog," I said, "I don't have any money and even if I did, you can't charge me to climb into my own bed. Have a heart, will you? I'm in a bad mood, so back off, okay?"

To my surprise, Mad Dog backed off. Well, not entirely. He did try to kick my feet out from under me as I climbed up into my bunk, but at least he didn't charge me to get into my own bed. Maybe his teeth weren't bothering him that much at the time.

Mr. Mootz came in the cabin and blew a loud whistle.

"Lunchtime in half an hour, boys. Get your gear

stored and meet outside in fifteen minutes," he said. Then he blew the whistle again. That was going to get old very quickly.

Lunch was burnt grilled-cheese sandwiches and lumpy tomato soup. For dessert there was fresh fruit. A lot of kids complained about that, but since dessert isn't a big thing in my house, I was fine with just a peach. At least it wasn't burnt or lumpy.

After we'd cleared our plates, we went outside and sat on the ground under the big flagpole with Mrs. West.

"This afternoon we're going to get a tour of the campgrounds," she told us. "Then I will take the girls, and Mr. Mootz will take the boys, down to the swamp for Critter Catch."

"I hope we catch some big slimy snakes," said Mad Dog loudly. "I bet there are lots of them in the swamp."

All the girls squealed and said "ewwwww" and the boys clapped and whooped even though I'm sure at least half of them were just as scared at the thought of running into a big snake as the girls were.

The tour of the campgrounds took about an hour.

Like our cabins, everything had a special camp name. The dining hall was called, "Sequoia," the bathrooms were called "Lily Pads," the meeting place under the flagpole was "Toadstool," and the camp nurse's office — just in case the cutesy names made anybody sick — was called "Aloe."

The only good part was seeing Mount Wood. It was even taller and more impressive than in the pictures we'd seen. Standing there next to it, looking up, everyone got quiet. I wasn't sure if it was because they were scared, or like me, they were excited just thinking about the big race.

The only bad thing about seeing the tower was that it made me miss Fink even more. I don't think Fink would have climbed Mount Wood (it really was big), but he would have coached me, and I know he would have been really happy for me if I won the race. It would have been great to have been the "Mount Woodsters."

Critter Catch might not have been so bad, except that Mr. Mootz brought his puppets with him and he kept up a running dialogue with them about everything we dragged out of the muck.

"Oh, will you look at that, Doozy! Nate's caught another salamander. Hooray for Nate! Hooray for the salamander! Hooray for today!"

I knew she wasn't a real person — she was a sock — but I was really starting to dislike Doozy. For one thing, no matter how many times I told her my name was Nat, not Nate, she couldn't seem to get it right.

The girls were on the other side of the swamp with Mrs. West, but we could hear them screaming every now and then. The only thing worse than a girl screaming is a whole bunch of girls screaming.

Mad Dog didn't catch a snake, but he did make me jump about a mile once by tickling the back of my leg with a weed and making a hissing noise. It was going to be a very long week for me, that much I could already tell.

That night at dinner, somehow I ended up sitting at the same table as Jessie. She looked just as miserable as I felt, sitting there pushing soggy macaroni and cheese around on her plate.

"Did you catch anything at Critter Catch?" she asked me.

"A couple of salamanders," I said.

"Not me. Everybody was screaming so much they scared everything over to your side of the pond. I didn't even get to catch one crummy thing," she complained.

I was surprised to hear that Jessie hadn't been one of the screamers. Somehow I hadn't pictured her being the critter-catching type.

"At least you didn't have puppets talking to you the whole time," I said.

"Yeah, I can't stand that Doozy," she said. "She's WAY too cheerful."

I was just about to agree when Mrs. West stood up and clinked her glass with a knife.

"Attention, everybody! Attention, please!" Everyone quieted down and listened. "What a wonderful first day we've had. We all enjoyed the Critter Catch, though perhaps the girls should take a lesson from the boys and keep the decibel level down next time if they want to catch anything."

The boys whooped triumphantly. Then Mrs. West told us that the next day we would start working on our science projects with our partners. Jessie and I exchanged a look. I wondered what that was going to be like, but I didn't think about it too hard since I was already bummed out enough.

It was too late for us to have a campfire or anything that night; plus, we were all pretty pooped, so we just went back to our cabins and went to sleep. Even Mad Dog was too tired to bug me. At least not while he was awake. Once he was asleep, his snoring was so loud it almost blew me out of the bunk. The only thing worse than his snoring was the mosquitoes trying to dive-bomb me, but I finally managed to go to sleep by putting my pillow over my head and jamming my fingers in my ears.

When I woke up the next morning, I opened my eyes and my heart almost stopped dead in my chest! There was a swamp monster standing next to my bed, breathing its foul breath all over me. I sat up so fast I banged my head on the ceiling. Grabbing my pants from the end of the bed, I jammed my legs into them and got ready to run for my life.

CHAPTER TEN

"Not schow fashst," said the monster in its strange, wet, slurred voice. "You wanna get down fwom there, itsch gonna cosht you two arm sschlugs."

It was Mad Dog. I hadn't recognized him in his headgear. My mom makes some kids with braces wear headgear at night if they have what's called an underbite. I guess Mad Dog has one, because he was wearing the headgear. It's a complicated-looking contraption that goes in your mouth and is held on by straps that go behind your ears and over your head.

He may not have been a swamp monster, but he definitely had swamp monster breath.

"What's an arm slug?" I asked him groggily.

To demonstrate, he stood on the edge of his bunk, reached over the railing, and punched me hard in the upper arm.

"OW!" I shouted.

"Hey, be quiet, you guys!" Danny Lebson grumbled from his bunk. "I'm trying to sleep."

"Oh, sorry to disturb your beauty rest," I said sarcastically. "I'll try to be quieter from now on while I'm being tortured."

"That'shs one," said Mad Dog. "And here'schs two." He pounded my arm again.

"OW!" I shouted.

"Come on!" came an angry chorus of sleepy voices. "Knock it off."

Mad Dog does not like being told what to do, and to make sure everybody would remember that, he grabbed a tube of toothpaste out of his bag and ran around the cabin squirting big sticky gobs of peppermint paste in everyone's hair.

Just as Mad Dog was about to squirt me, Mr. Mootz

bounded into the room blowing his whistle. Doozy and Dontsy were on his hands and he had put little shirts and hats on them.

"Rise and shine, pals o' mine!" he chirped in his high, cheerful Doozy voice. "Get out of bed, or I'll bop your head," he added in Dontsy's grumbling voice.

I couldn't believe it, but between the arm slugs, the whistle blowing, the toothpaste attacks, and the horrible hand puppets, I couldn't wait to get out of there and find Jessie so we could get started on our project. This was definitely a first — me looking forward to spending time with Corn Bloomers.

After breakfast we all met under the flagpole (which I just couldn't bring myself to call "Toadstool") again and Mrs. West gave us our instructions.

"You've had your time in the library and on the Internet back at school to prepare your research. Now the exciting part begins. Fieldwork," she said. "Please make use of the natural facilities to collect as much data for your projects as you can. We'll meet back at Sequoia at noon for lunch. Off you go!"

Everybody ran off in different directions. Jessie and I just stood there and looked at each other.

"Where should we go?" I asked.

"How should I know? This was your *brilliant* idea," she said sarcastically.

"Hey, you said yesterday you thought it was an interesting idea. Don't be taking that back now," I said.

"Don't be telling me what to do," she said, sitting down on the ground and starting to pull up little clumps of grass with her fingers.

So much for this being better than the whistle blowing and the hand puppets.

"Look, I don't want to work with you any more than you want to work with me, Jessie," I said, "but we're stuck with each other."

"Don't remind me," she said without looking up. "I'm trying to forget."

"I'm warning you. I'm in a really bad mood," I said.

"I'm in a worse one," she told me.

Great, now we were going to compete over who was grumpier.

"Fine. You want to just sit there pulling up grass and complaining about your mood? It's okay with me," I said, flopping down on the ground and lying back with my arms crossed behind my head. "I really don't care. So what if we don't do any research? Mrs. West can go ahead and flunk us. I've had it with Camp Willomet."

"Ouch!" Jessie said all of a sudden. "Ouch! Ouch! OUCH!" She jumped up and started dancing around, slapping at her bare legs.

"What's the matter?" I asked, jumping up, too.

"Something's biting me!" she cried.

I looked down where she'd been sitting. There was a big flat rock, and running all over it were a bunch of ants.

"Perfect!" I shouted.

"Oooh, you are so mean, Nat Boyd," Jessie shouted. "How could you say that when I'm in pain?"

"Wait! I don't mean perfect about the bites. I mean perfect about the ants. I think when you sat on them you disturbed the nest. Come back over here and look at this, will you?"

Jessie came over to where I was squatting on the ground.

"Big deal. It's a rock with some ants on it, some of which just bit me," Jessie said, rubbing the red marks on her legs. "If that's an ant nest, where are the princesses? Where are the princes? Where's all the good stuff?"

"It's not the right time of year for the princesses," I explained. "It's not warm enough yet."

"Hey," she said, squinching up her beady little eyes at me. "You tricked me! You said we were going to see an ant wedding. Otherwise, I never would have given up on tree rings so easily."

"Get me a stick," I said.

"Get it yourself," she told me.

I went and got a long stick.

"Watch this," I said.

Carefully, I began to poke the stick at the rock. I moved it a little, and the ants on top of the rock went crazy.

"What are you doing?" Jessie cried, grabbing the stick out of my hands. "This is supposed to be a science project, not some silly boy thing like scaring poor, defenseless, little ants."

I didn't bother to point out that she'd called those same poor, defenseless, little ants *pests* just the other day. I grabbed the stick back from her.

"Calm down and watch, will you?" I said.

Carefully, I worked the stick under the edge of the rock and then with a sudden push, I flipped it over, revealing the nest.

"Wow! Look at them all," Jessie said, leaning over to study the nest. "What are all those little holes for?"

"They're tunnels," I said, "leading down to the queen and the nursery."

Jessie looked at me with wide eyes.

"The nursery?" she said.

"Yep, that's where they keep the ant babies. See, here comes a worker ant out of that hole right now!" I said, excitedly pointing to a little ant with a smooth white oval thing in its jaws.

"What's that thing it's carrying?" Jessie asked.

"It's a cocoon. There's a baby ant in there."

For the next two hours, Jessie and I sat by the nest

and watched the ants. We saw worker ants, and guard ants, and all different stages of baby ants. We saw ants bringing food back to the nest, and we even saw a couple of ant fights. Seeing them up close and real like that was even better than the stuff I'd watched about ants on TV, or read about in the books at school.

Jessie, who's a pretty good artist, had a pad and colored pencils with her, so she drew pictures and we took notes on what we saw.

"Do you think we'll see the queen?" Jessie asked me.

"I'm not sure. She's probably down there pretty deep in the nest," I said. "I wouldn't want to dig around too much. They're probably already pretty unhappy about us taking the rock off."

"Maybe we should put it back," Jessie said.

"Oh, we will. Now that we know where they are, we can just take the rock off when we want to watch, and put it back on when we're finished."

Time whizzed by and twelve o'clock came before we knew it. All the kids came running back with their butterfly nets and specimen jars full of worms and bugs. Everyone seemed excited, but I doubted that anybody had discovered anything as great as our ant nest. Mad Dog was carrying a big empty jar, and he was all covered with mud. David was muddy, too, and they both looked pretty unhappy.

"No luck, Mr. Framer?" asked Mrs. West.

David shook his head.

"We thought maybe we saw something, but it turned out to be a stick," he said.

"Good-for-nothin' swamp doesn't have nothin' in it today," Mad Dog grumbled.

"Looks like *you* were in it today," Jessie said.

I was surprised she had the nerve to insult him like that. I know I wouldn't have.

Jessie sat at a big table with some other girls, but she came over to me in the middle of lunch.

"Hurry up and finish your sandwich so we can get back out there and see what they're doing," she said.

I gulped down my tuna fish sandwich in about

three bites, grabbed an apple from the middle of the table, and we took off. I was just as eager as she was to see what the ants were up to.

"Hey, slow down, you two!" Mrs. West laughed as we rushed past her. "Where are you going?"

"We've got an appointment to see the queen," Jessie said, and we both laughed.

When we got back to the nest, we stopped dead in our tracks. It wasn't the way we'd left it. The rock, which we'd carefully put back on the nest, was thrown to the side, a couple of feet away, and the nest itself was ruined! Somebody had stomped all over it. There wasn't an ant in sight.

Jessie burst into tears. I usually hate it when girls cry, but this time I didn't blame her. I felt like crying myself. Instead, I took a couple of quick, angry bites of my apple and stared at the ground.

"Who did this?" she asked. "Who would do something this awful?"

I was about to say I didn't know, when something I hadn't noticed before suddenly jumped out at me.

Solid proof! I took a last bite of my apple, and tossed the core on the ground.

"Hey, don't litter," said Jessie, pointing to the core.

"Don't worry about it, it's biodegradable," I said as I turned and headed back toward the dining hall. "Come on! I know who ruined the nest, and this time, *he's* the one who's gonna pay the price."

CHAPTER ELEVEN

"Prove it!" shouted Mad Dog, pushing his chair back from the table and standing up.

"Come outside and I will!" I shouted back.

"What on earth is going on here?" Mrs. West said as she came rushing over to the table where Jessie and I were arguing with Mad Dog.

"Mad Dog wrecked our ant nest, Mrs. West. He stomped all over it," Jessie said, fighting back tears. "He killed all the babies."

"I did not!" shouted Mad Dog. "You can't prove anything."

"Oh, yes, we can," Jessie said. "Can't we, Nat?"

Suddenly, it was as though someone turned off

the lights and I couldn't see the people around me anymore. And I couldn't hear them, either. All I heard was Fink's voice talking to me in my head.

"Think, Natalie. Think!" he said. "If Mad Dog gets kicked out of camp because of you, he'll never let you forget it. He'll hate you forever. Forever, Natalie. Are you paying attention? *Forever . . .*" The voice trailed off and the lights came back on. Everyone was looking at me.

"Well?" said Jessie. "Can we prove it or not?"

"No," I said. "We can't. Just forget about it."

"Are you sure you don't want to tell me what happened?" Mrs. West asked.

"I'm sure," I said. "It's nothing."

That was that. Mad Dog sat back down and he and everyone else went back to finishing their lunches. Jessie gave me the squinchiest look ever and stormed out of the lodge.

"Wait up!" I said, running after her.

"Why should I? You're such a wimp. How could you say it was nothing? Mad Dog wrecked our nest and you just let him get away with it," she yelled at me.

"What good would it do to tell on him?" I said. "There's no use crying over spilt milk."

"You and those corny expressions!" said Jessie with a snort. "Why should we let him get away with it? He wrecked the nest. He should get in trouble."

"You don't understand," I told her. "He's not the one who would get in trouble."

"Oh, I get it. All you're worried about is yourself. You're afraid of him, aren't you? That's what this is all about. You're scared of Mad Dog," she said. "Why don't you just admit it already? You're scared of him."

I didn't wait for the lights to dim this time or for Fink's voice to tell me not to do what I was about to do. I knew the time had come. I was tired of trying to hide it.

"Okay, fine. You're right. I'm afraid of him. Are you happy now? You finally got me to say it," I said. "I'm afraid of Mad Dog."

Jessie's mouth fell open in shock.

"You're admitting it?" she said after a few seconds. "*To me*? You never would have done that in a million years if Fink was here."

"Well, he's not here, is he? So go ahead and tease me if you want," I said. "Mad Dog is twice my size, he's blaming me for his braces, and he's charging me arm slugs to get in and out of my own bed. Sorry, but my life is hard enough already. I don't want to make it even worse by getting him kicked out of camp."

Jessie was quiet for a minute.

"What's an arm slug?" she finally asked.

"What do you care?" I asked grumpily. "He's not going to do it to *you*."

"You're right. He probably won't ever give me arm slugs," she said. "But he might have."

Then she did something that totally shocked me, and was so weird and embarrassing that I wondered for a second whether I was actually dreaming. Instead of making fun of me, Jessie Kornblume hugged me. In real life it probably only lasted a couple of seconds, but it seemed like forever.

"Why'd you do that?" I asked when it was finally over.

"Because you saved me from Mad Dog," she said.

"I did?" I said, looking around nervously, hoping nobody had seen what just happened.

"Yeah, I was the one who told Mrs. West it was him. If he had gotten kicked out of camp, he would have blamed me, not you."

"Let's get one thing straight," I said. "I may have saved you, but I didn't do it on purpose. So don't go thinking I like you or anything disgusting like that."

"Don't worry, I won't," said Jessie. "And in case you're wondering, I don't like you or anything disgusting like that, either."

"Cool," I said, breathing a sigh of relief.

"How did you know it was Mad Dog, anyway?" Jessie asked.

"The footprints," I said. "I recognized the waffle pattern from the soles of his shoes. I saw them once when he was sitting in my mom's office chair."

"Pretty clever," she said.

We walked over to the place where the nest had been, so I could show Jessie the prints.

"Do you think the ants are all dead?" she asked, looking sadly at the stomped ground. "Even the queen?"

"Probably," I said. "Those are pretty big boots."

"It's my fault, you know," she said softly. "If I hadn't said that thing about Mad Dog being in the swamp, he wouldn't have stomped on the nest."

"Oh, I don't know. Maybe his teeth were hurting and he did it to get back at me," I said. "There's no point in blaming yourself."

Jessie took a step back and put both hands on her hips.

"Why are you being so nice to me all of a sudden?" she demanded.

I honestly wasn't sure why. Maybe it was because she cared about the ant nest as much as I did. Or because she hated Doozy for being too cheerful. Or maybe it was because I knew she missed Marla as much as I missed Fink. But before I could even figure out if I wanted to try to put any of that into words, she pointed to the ground and shouted, "Look at that!"

She was pointing at my apple core, lying on the ground near the old nest site.

"I told you already, it's *biodegradable*," I said. "You *do* know what that means, don't you, Miss Farnsworth Aptitude test?" I said.

"Don't insult me, you airhead. Of course I do. But look at the apple. There are ants all over it!" she said.

She was right. We squatted down on the ground and watched as the ants gathered bits of apple in their jaws.

"Let's watch where they go," Jessie whispered excitedly.

As we watched, a tiny trail of ants, carrying their food, headed right back to the place where the nest had originally been. What we saw next made us both smile.

"They've made a new hole! And look, those guys over there are working on another one," I said.

"Those *girls*, you mean," said Jessie.

"Mad Dog only messed up the top, so the rest of the nest must still be okay," I said.

If Fink had been there, we would have whooped and hollered and clapped each other on the back. That's what boys do when they're happy about something. Somehow, I didn't feel like clapping Jessie on the back, though, and I certainly didn't want to hug her. It was bad enough that she'd hugged me. I wasn't about to do it back. So instead, I punched her in the arm.

"Ow! What was that for?" she asked, rubbing her arm in surprise.

"You said you wanted to know what an arm slug was," I said. "So now you know."

"Boys are *so* weird," she said, shaking her head. Then, even though I'd punched her, she smiled at me and I smiled back.

That afternoon there was something called "Woods Walk" planned, but Jessie and I got permission from Mrs. West to stay behind. We wanted to watch the ants rebuild their nest.

We sat there together, happily watching the ants

until everybody came back from the hike. Mad Dog didn't come over to us or say anything. He knew that we knew he was the one who had stomped on the nest. I guess maybe he was afraid that we might change our minds about pointing the finger at him. As it turned out, we didn't have to. Mad Dog got himself kicked out of camp all by himself the next day.

CHAPTER TWELVE

"How could you do this, young man? How could you destroy private property like this?" Mr. Mootz demanded. He was so angry his face was red, and behind his glasses his eyes looked like they were ready to pop right out of his head.

"My feet were cold," Mad Dog replied, carefully avoiding making eye contact with Mootz.

"So why didn't you put on a pair of your *own* socks?" Mootz asked.

"It was dark in here. How was I supposed to know they weren't my socks?" Mad Dog said, doing a lousy job of trying to sound innocent.

"They had arms and legs and faces sewn on them.

Do your socks have arms and legs and faces on them?" Mootz asked, and I wondered if he was going to cry.

It was obvious that Mad Dog was lying. First of all, there's no way you could mistake Doozy and Dontsy for regular socks. Like Mootz said, they had arms and legs attached to them, which you would definitely notice if you tried to put them on your feet, even in the dark. Second, everybody knew that Mootz kept the puppets in a special box under his bunk. We'd all seen him putting them away at night. Mad Dog's bunk was all the way across the room from Mootz's. It's not like Mad Dog could have been fishing around for his socks in the dark and found them by accident under Mootz's bed.

I think Mad Dog must have swiped the puppets early in the morning, while the rest of us were sleeping. Mootz noticed they were missing right away, because they weren't in the box when he got ready to do his little "rise and shine" routine. All day, Mootz worried about the missing puppets. He kept asking if anybody had seen them, but Mad Dog hadn't said a word. It wasn't until we were sitting around the campfire that night, toasting marshmallows, that Mootz noticed one of Doozy's little arms sticking out of the back of one of Mad Dog's boots.

That day, the third day of camp, the whole class had taken a day-long hike and canoe trip down the river. We'd climbed big rocks, walked through mud, and waded in the river catching minnows. Poor Doozy and Dontsy had gotten even more worn out by it than the rest of us had. Those socks were so filthy and smelly and full of holes, they were unrecognizable by the time Mr. Mootz pulled them off of Mad Dog's feet that night, back in the cabin.

Mr. Mootz didn't even wait until after lights-out to call Mad Dog's parents. We could all hear him yelling on the phone in the office. The next morning, before we'd even sat down to breakfast, Mrs. Ditmeyer arrived at camp to take Mad Dog home.

I certainly wasn't going to miss him, and even though I felt genuinely sorry for Mr. Mootz, I have to admit I was glad Doozy and Dontsy were gone, too. In a way, even though I'm sure he hadn't meant to, Mad Dog had done us all a favor.

*   *   *

The ants were doing a great job of rebuilding the nest. Jessie and I were keeping track of how many new holes they made each day and what kind of stuff they brought into the nest. Mrs. West stopped by that afternoon to see how our project was going and she seemed very impressed with the work we were doing.

"I smell an A," I told Jessie after she left.

"Maybe. But we need a good title for the project," she said, pulling out a sheet of paper on which she'd written something in fancy script. "What do you think of 'Formica Polyctena' by Jessie Kornblume and Nat Boyd?"

"What the heck does that mean?" I asked, looking at the strange words she'd written on the paper.

"That's the Latin name for red ants," she said, as if I was some kind of dummy and anybody with half a brain would know that.

"Why don't we just call it 'Red Ants,' since nobody we know, including us, speaks Latin?" I asked.

"Because 'Formica Polyctena' sounds more *scientific*," she said. "Mrs. West will like that better."

"Okay, fine. We can call it that, but only if you

change it so my name comes first at the bottom," I said. "It was my idea to do ants in the first place."

"Okay, I guess that's fair," she said, pulling out her eraser and handing it to me. "You do the erasing and then I'll rewrite it."

I was just thinking that even though we can't stand each other, Jessie and I made a pretty good team, then we heard a horn honk. At first, I thought maybe it was Mr. Mootz in his car again, but when I looked up, I couldn't believe who I saw sitting in the front seat of the red minivan that had just pulled up.

"Fink!" I shouted, dropping the eraser and running as fast as I could to the car.

"Natalie!" he yelled from the open window.

"What are you doing here?" I asked, grabbing the door handle and yanking it open.

"You said for me to get well soon, *or else*," he said. "You didn't think I'd just ignore that threat, did you?"

I laughed.

"No, really, how come you're here?" I asked.

"It was a false alarm. I didn't have tonsillitis, after all. Just a regular sore throat," he told me as he got out of the car and clapped me on the back. "I'm to- tally recovered."

"So, can you stay?" I asked.

"No, I had my dad drive me all the way up here just so I could look at your ugly face for a minute and then go home," he said. "Yeah, I can stay. What do you think?" He laughed and slid open the back door so he could get his stuff out.

I took his duffel bag for him and he carried his sleeping bag and pillow as I led him over to the boys' cabin. Mr. Fink went off to find Mrs. West to let her know Fink had arrived.

"So how is it here?" Fink asked me. "How's camp?"

"It's great," I said, instantly forgetting the crummy cabin, the lousy food, the arm slugs, the puppets, and the stomped ant nest.

"Follow me," I said. "The boys are in Yucca."

"Excuse me?" said Fink.

"That's our cabin's name, 'Yucca.' The girls are in 'Evergreen,'" I told him.

"How's Mount Wood?" he asked.

"I've only seen it so far. We don't get to climb it until tomorrow," I told him. "You got here just in time."

"I had to promise my mom I wouldn't climb it before she'd let me come today," Fink said. "My dad's delivering the note to Mrs. West right now."

"I won't climb it either, then," I said.

"Are you kidding?" Fink said. "You have to! We're a team. The 'Mount Woodsters,' remember? I figure if I coach and you win, that means I can claim half of the credit. So, have you been practicing?" he asked.

I shook my head.

"Too busy watching ants. Jessie and I found the coolest nest," I said. "Wait 'til you see it."

Fink stopped walking and stood still.

"Did I just hear you right? Did you say, *Jessie* and you found the nest?" he said, slowly turning toward me. "Since when do you do anything with Jessie other than avoid or insult her?"

"Since you and Marla couldn't come to camp, Mrs. West told us we had to be science project partners," I said.

"Oh, Nat-o. I am SO sorry," he said, throwing an arm over my shoulder. "Are you okay? I'm surprised you haven't killed each other by now."

"Actually, it's been fine," I said. "Jessie drew some really great pictures of the ants and we've been having a ball watching them. And you're not going to believe this, but I even admitted to her that I was scared of Mad Dog."

"You did?" Fink asked. "Did she give you a hard time?"

"Nope. She hasn't really said anything about it. I'm telling you, it's weird, but she's not so bad without Marla around," I said.

"Really? Well, if you're having such a good time with Jessie, your new best friend, maybe I should just pack my stuff back up and go home," he said.

At first I thought he was serious, but then he started laughing, so I laughed, too. It was great to see him again. I couldn't believe he was actually there. Fink and me at nature camp, just like we'd always talked about.

While I helped Fink unpack his junk, I told him about what had happened to Mad Dog.

"You mean he actually wore those annoying puppets on his feet?" he said. "You gotta admit that takes a lot of nerve."

I was about to describe the look on Mr. Mootz's face when I heard someone behind us clear her throat.

"Eh-hem!"

It was Jessie. She was standing in the doorway of our cabin with her arms crossed and her foot tapping. She was furious.

"What do you think you're doing?" she demanded.

"I'm helping Fink unpack. What's it look like I'm doing?" I said.

"It looks like you're doing what you boys always do. Leaving all the work to me and then running around taking credit for it," she said.

"Thanks for the warm welcome," Fink said.

"You're welcome," Jessie said, ignoring him. "In case you forgot, we have work to do, Nat. I'm going back to the nest, and if you're not there in two minutes to finish that erasing, I'm leaving my name first on the title page and I'm doing it in ink, too."

She left and Fink just stared at me.

"She sounds just like my mom when she's yelling at my dad," he said.

"I guess she's mad," I said.

"So let her be," said Fink. "Let's go find something high for you to jump off of. We don't have much time. We've got to get you in shape for tomorrow."

I didn't know what to do.

"Um, I should kind of go back and help her. We're counting ant holes," I said. "It's part of the project. We're making a chart."

Fink just stared at me.

"You're kidding, right? You want to hang out with Jessie and a bunch of ants instead of me?" he said. "And by the way, Nat-Man, you're scratching your knee, in case you haven't noticed."

For once, I knew exactly why my knee was itching. No matter what I did now, someone was going to be mad at me.

CHAPTER THIRTEEN

"Come on," I said to Fink. "Let's go."

"Cool," said Fink.

He tossed his sleeping bag onto Mad Dog's old bunk and followed me out of the cabin and down the path that led through the woods toward the main part of camp. I pointed out things as we went.

"Over there is the swamp where we had Critter Catch, and there's the river where we went canoeing yesterday — and Mad Dog wiped out Doozy and Dontsy — and that's the fire ring where we toasted marshmallows last night."

"What's that?" asked Fink, pointing over at the far edge of the woods.

"*That's* Mount Wood," I said.

"Sweet!" Fink cried. "Just think, Nat-Man, tomorrow you're going to grab the glory up there for the Mount Woodsters, and go down in Camp Willomet history forever. Maybe you can even set a new speed record."

"You think?" I asked.

"Totally," said Fink. "Who else has a personal coach? It's a huge advantage."

As we walked, I did my best to catch him up on some of the important things he'd missed about camp so far. " 'Lily Pads' are bathrooms, 'Toadstool' is the meeting place under the flagpole, and 'Sequoia' is the dining hall," I explained.

"Do I *have* to call it a 'Lily Pad'?" he asked.

"Don't worry," I told him. "You'll get used to it."

"What's that big log building over there?" Fink asked, pointing at Sequoia.

"That's where we're going," I said. "Come on. I want to show you something."

I felt a little nervous as I led Fink up the path and over the little bridge to Sequoia.

"Oh, great. What's *he* doing here?" Jessie asked as we walked up to where she was squatting by the nest, drawing on her pad.

"I want to show him what we've been doing," I said.

Jessie didn't say anything. She just stood up and crossed her arms again, squinching up her eyes at us.

"See, this is what I was talking about, Fink. Jessie found the nest by accident. Then Mad Dog tried to wreck it and now they're rebuilding it."

Fink got down on his hands and knees and looked closely at the nest.

"Hey, this is pretty cool. Look at that little guy! Look at the way he's carrying that huge grain of rice around like it's nothing," Fink said, pointing to one of the ants. "It's just like you said, Nat-o, fifty times their own weight."

"For your information, that grain of rice is a cocoon and that guy is a girl. They're all girls. Funny how the girls do all the work, huh?" said Jessie.

"You know, Corn Bloomers, you weren't supposed to be working on this project at all. Nat and I were the ones who were supposed to do it," Fink said. "You were going to do tree rings with Marla, re-member?"

Jessie's eyes suddenly filled up with tears.

"Creep," she said.

Fink gave me one of those "What did I do?" kind of looks.

I shrugged. Who knew why she was so upset?

"Girls," said Fink, shaking his head. "They're all cuckoo in the coconut."

He got up and was dusting himself off when Mrs. West and his dad came out of the camp office — better known as "Wigwam." Mr. Fink motioned for Fink to come over and say good-bye to him. So he left.

"What's the matter?" I asked as soon as Fink was gone. "Why are you acting so weird all of sudden?"

"Why are you?" she said.

"I'm not acting weird," I said.

"Yes, you are. You were being all nice and every-thing before, and we were working on the project and having fun, and then all of a sudden you just walked away and left me there without even saying any-thing," she said.

"Well, Fink got here. What was I supposed to do?" I said.

"You could have told him you were busy," she said.

"Oh, like you would've done that if Marla suddenly showed up and you were so happy to see her, you just about busted open?" I said. "Get real."

Now she really looked like she was going to cry. The last time that had happened, I ended up getting hugged and I definitely didn't want to go through *that* again.

"I take it back," I said quickly. "I'm sorry. Look, whatever I said, I didn't mean it. Just, whatever you do, don't cry again, okay?"

"You don't get it, do you?" she said as two fat tears slipped out and rolled slowly down her cheeks. "Even though it was bad at first, everything was sort of okay because it was even, and then for a while it was actually fine, but now it's lopsided and that feels even worse than it did before."

I wasn't exactly sure what she was trying to say, but I had a feeling it had something to do with Fink coming back and Marla still being home sick. And when I thought about it, I realized that if it had happened the other way around, and it had been Marla instead of Fink who'd showed up, I probably would have felt bad, too.

So when Fink finished saying good-bye to his dad, I went over and we had a little talk. At first he didn't get what I was saying at all.

"Why do you care if she's bent out of shape about some silly old science project?" he asked.

"I don't think it's that," I said. "I think she feels weird about you coming back."

"Well, like I said back at the cabin, Nat-o, if you two want to be alone, just let me know. I'm happy to go home," he said, and this time he wasn't laughing.

"Quit being dumb," I said.

"Go suck your *thumb*," said Fink.

I guess it couldn't be too bad if Fink wanted to play the rhyming game with me.

"Don't step on the *ants*," I said.

"Go wet your *pants*," Fink said.

I laughed. Fink and I were fine. But then I looked

over at Jessie, who was still standing over by the nest sniffling, and I bent down and scratched my knee.

"Calm down and quit scratching," said Fink. "Everything is going to be fine. I've got an idea."

"You do?" I asked.

"Of course," said Fink.

"You're the best," I told him.

"I'm glad you remember," he said.

"Are you sure?" Jessie asked, when Fink finished telling her his idea.

"Yeah," he said. "The deal is, if you let me work on the ant project with you and Nat, then you can be one of the 'Mount Woodsters.'"

"And you're going to coach me?" Jessie asked Fink. "I'd be on the team for real?"

"Yep," he said.

Just like I hadn't thought Jessie would be into Critter Catching, it hadn't even occurred to me that she would want to climb Mount Wood. But boy, did she ever! We spent the rest of the afternoon together, the three of us. Jessie and I filled Fink in on every-thing we'd learned about the ants and their nest so far. Then after dinner, Fink started coaching. He made Jessie and me do stretches first, and then we climbed a bunch of trees while he yelled at us from below about going faster and not looking down.

"You gotta give it everything you've got on the way up, you guys," he told us, "because when it's time to come down, it's all up to gravity."

Jessie worked really hard, and we both definitely improved with Fink's coaching.

"Looking good," I called out to her after a partic-ularly fast climb.

She smiled and pushed up her glasses.

"You too," she called back to me.

We both skinned our knees pretty badly rubbing against the rough bark of the trees as we climbed, and I could tell that Fink was impressed that Jessie didn't make a fuss about it.

"See what I mean?" I whispered to him at one point. "She's better without her evil twin around."

On Friday morning, the last day of camp, I woke

up early. Fink was still sleeping underneath me in his bunk, but I was too excited to sleep anymore. I couldn't wait to climb Mount Wood! I kept picturing that bronze plaque with my name on it.

I heard a noise outside the cabin and peeked out the window. Jessie was standing out there. She saw me and motioned for me to come out.

"Is Fink awake yet?" she whispered. "I want to get in a little more practice before the race."

"He's still sleeping, but we can do it on our own, don't you think?" I asked her.

We walked into the woods, found a couple of good climbing trees and quickly scrambled up.

"I know you're going to beat me in the race," she said.

I was pretty sure I was a stronger climber than Jessie, but she was totally fearless about the jumping.

"You could win," I told her, "especially if I choke when it's time to get down."

"Wouldn't it be cool if we tied?" she asked.

Truthfully, I thought it would be cooler if I won, but I didn't want to tell her that.

"Yeah, that would be cool," I said.

"If either of us wins, it will be like all of us winning, though, because we're a team," she said.

"Yeah," I said. "The 'Mount Woodsters.' Come on, let's get in a couple more climbs before breakfast."

After we finished climbing, Jessie went back to Evergreen to get something.

"It's a surprise," she told me.

I went back to my cabin, too, and waited around for Fink to get dressed so we could walk over to Sequoia together for breakfast.

"Do you feel ready?" he asked me.

"Nervous. But yeah, I'm ready," I said.

Jessie was waiting for us at the lodge with her "surprise." It was three white T-shirts with MOUNT WOODSTERS written on them. She'd used a black marker to make them the night before in her cabin. She was wearing hers already.

"Since we are a team, we ought to look like a team, too, right?" she asked, handing us our shirts.

"Uh, gee, Jessie," stammered Fink. "You shouldn't have."

I knew, without having to ask, that Fink wasn't any more interested in wearing matching shirts than I was, but neither one of us wanted to hurt Jessie's feelings. So we said thanks, and tried not to look sick to our stomachs as we put on the shirts. Luckily, they were way too small for us.

"Can't you at least *try* to wear them?" Jessie asked. "Maybe they'll stretch."

But Fink convinced Jessie that it would be a bad idea for me to wear anything tight to climb in, and that it would be impossible for him to coach right if he couldn't wave his arms around comfortably. Fortunately, she bought it, and we didn't have to wear the shirts.

After breakfast we headed over to Mount Wood for the big race. Mr. Volmer, the camp guy, was there to be the official timer. Everyone was very excited. Quite a few kids were going to race, and everybody else had come to watch.

Two people were allowed to climb at a time. Jessie and I volunteered to go first. Up close, Mount Wood seemed taller than ever and my heart thumped and banged against my ribs as I put on my helmet, strapped on the harness, and got ready to climb. When Mr. Volmer blew the whistle, Fink started shouting directions at us.

"Move your legs, Jessie! Keep those elbows in, Nat! Go, team, go!" he yelled.

Everybody cheered and clapped when I reached the top. I didn't know how long it had taken me to get up, but I felt like I'd climbed faster than I ever had before. I'd seen Jessie slip once on the way up, which had slowed her down some. She reached the top of the platform just as I strapped on the bungee cord and got ready to jump down.

"Come on, Nat-o-matic! Jump!" I heard Fink yelling.

I wanted to jump. I wanted to win the race, but when I looked down over the edge of the platform, suddenly everything seemed to be swirling. I felt dizzy and a little sick.

"Close your eyes, Nat," I heard Jessie say. "We'll jump together on three." She had her cord attached and was standing next to me.

"I'm not sure I can do it," I said nervously.

"Yes, you can," she told me. "One, two, three!"

She grabbed hold of my hand and the next thing I knew I was falling. I let go of Jessie's hand and looked over at her. Her red hair was flying up in the air behind her. She laughed and gave me a thumbs-up. Before I could do it back, we'd landed in the foam padding.

"Incredible!" she cried.

"Amazing!" I said, standing up on wobbly legs.

"Sweet!" shouted Fink, who had come over to congratulate us on our jump.

"Who landed first?" Jessie asked.

"You jumped at the same time, but I'm pretty sure Nat's feet hit the ground first," Fink told us, "probably because he's heavier."

"I knew you'd beat me," Jessie said.

She sounded a little disappointed, and I was surprised to find that now I really did wish we'd tied.

"I wouldn't have beat you if you hadn't helped me jump," I said.

I don't think I could have climbed Mount Wood

any faster than I did that day, and although according to Mr. Volmer I did beat Jessie by one and a half seconds, I didn't win the race. David Framer had the fastest time. I came in second and Jessie was a very close third.

"It would have meant the silver and bronze medals if this had been the Olympics," Fink said. "Not too shabby, if you ask me."

I was sad when it was time to get on the bus and leave Camp Willomet. In the short time he'd been there, Fink had gotten into being at the camp, too. I even heard him say he had to visit the "Lily Pad" once. It was especially hard to leave the ant nest behind. It would have been nice if we'd been able to stick around long enough to see the princes and princesses come out of the nest and fly away. Fink and Jessie and I went over there together to give it one last look before we got on the bus.

"Do you think they'll miss us, too?" Jessie asked.

I could tell by the look on Fink's face he was about to make fun of her for saying something sappy like that, but I jabbed him hard in the ribs before he could say anything.

Later, on the bus, when Jessie was sitting in Mad Dog's old seat next to David Framer, and Fink and I were sharing a seat of our own, Fink asked me why I'd poked him like that before.

"I was only going to zing her a little for getting corny about the ants," he said.

"Trust me, it wouldn't have been a smart thing to do," I said.

"Why not?" he asked.

"Because you might have made her cry and I happen to know that sometimes after girls cry they want to hug you," I told him.

Fink's eyes got wide.

"Really? How do you know that?" he asked.

"I'll tell you later," I said.

And of course, I did.

NAT'S MOM'S CORNY EXPRESSIONS

How many of Nat's mom's corny expressions can you fill in? Look back through the book to find them. Jot down the page number on the blank line, too.

There's more than _____ way

to skin a _____. _____

Strike while the _____ is _____. _____

Barking dogs seldom _____. _____

Every _____ has a _____ lining. _____

No _____, no _____. _____

Where there's _____, there's _____. _____

An _____ a _____ keeps the

_____ away. _____

There's no use _____ over _____
milk. _____

ABOUT THE AUTHOR

Sarah Weeks has written numerous picture books and novels, including *Mrs. McNosh Hangs up Her Wash; Two Eggs, Please; Follow the Moon;* and the popular Regular Guy series for middle-grade readers. *My Guy*, the third in that series, is currently in production at Disney for a feature-length, live-action film.

Ms. Weeks is a singer/songwriter as well as an author. Many of her books, such as *Angel Face, Crocodile Smile,* and *Without You,* include CDs of her original songs. She visits many schools and libraries throughout the country every year, speaking at assemblies and serving as author-in-residence. She lives in New York City with her two teenage sons.